W9-CJE-152

CHERRY

CHERRY
By
Booth Tarkington
ILLUSTRATED
HARPER & BROTHERS
PUBLISHERS NEW YORK & LONDON
1903
ROBERT MURRAY WRIGHT
1903

Published October, 1903

To the diligent and industrious members of the class of 1893 at Nassau Hall; also to the idler spirits who wasted the Golden Hours of Youth in profitless playing of toss-the-ball; and even to those more dissolute ones who risked the tutor's detection at pitch-the-penny and carved their names on Adam's table—in brief, to all of that happy class is dedicated this heroic tale of the days when Commencement came in September.

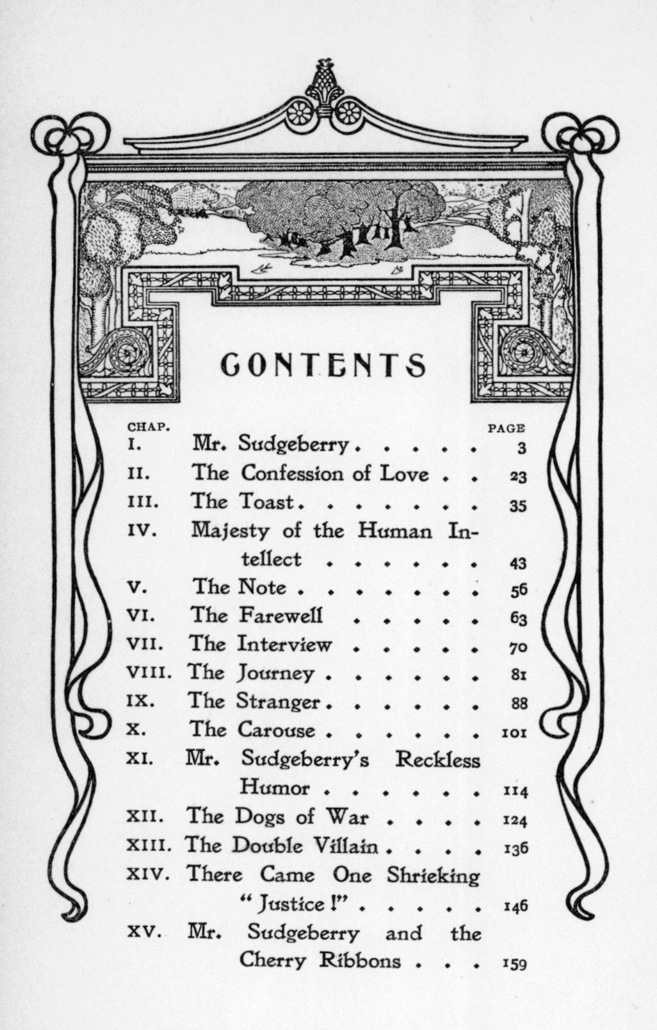

CONTENTS

ILLUSTRATIONS

CHERRY

MR. SUDGEBERRY

ACROSS the most vital precincts of the mind a flippant sprite of memory will sometimes skip, to the dismay of all philosophy. So it was with me no longer ago than last night; for, as I sat engaged in the composition of a treatise upon a subject worthy of the profoundest concentration, there suddenly fluttered before my mental eye some cherry-colored ribbons; and, quite inexplicably, at the same time, it became clear to me that the most charming morning of my life was that sunshiny one, in 1762, when Miss Sylvia Gray and I went walking.

It may be there are some who will declare that an aging person would do better to get forward with his treatise than to waste the treasure of his talent upon a narrative of the follies of youth; but this I refute. The flicker of cherry color having caused my pen to wander and me to have dreams all night —I never dream—what better than to seek relief by setting down the bewildering circumstances connected with the ribbons? Let me say that I have found through many experiences that writing out a thing works to lighten the burden of it, as a full-worded person must be bled of his words, or they coagulate within him and choke the veins of his mind, a condition which, in my younger days, was often near bringing me to the very italics of suffering.

Very early on the sunshiny morning to which allusion has been made, I found Miss

Sylvia at her gate, waiting to take the walk she had promised me. It was then, even before we set out, that I noticed the ribbons she wore that day. The fact that I remember a detail of this insignificance so great a number of years after is the more uncommon because I do not think that at the time I particularly noticed the ribbons, my mind being occupied with considerations of the lady's mental and moral attributes. However, it may not be gainsaid that this twinkling of bright colors seemed to me most befitting her appearance.

I had arrived at my father's house in the country but two days before, repairing thither upon finishing my third year of study at Nassau Hall, and I had proceeded at once to renew my pleasing acquaintance with Miss Gray, an acquaintance begun in childhood on account of our parents being neighbors, and continued later because of various betokenings of a feeling of growing admiration and reciprocal regard, clearly apparent, I think, between the maiden and myself. There was another lady of the neighborhood, Miss Amelia Robbins, who attracted me by the delicacy of her appreciation of my attentions, but at the time of which I speak my greater pleasure was in Miss Sylvia's company—I might put it: my infinitely greater pleasure.

In candor, I hope that I am justified in stating that certain qualities I was admitted to possess must have appealed to her liking, a something thoughtful and philosophic, a leaning toward theologic earnestness, added to a contempt for the gayeties of the world, mingled with a particular cautiousness and a nice severity of habit—which attributes, I believe will be confessed, are unusual in a youth of nineteen. Moreover, my achievements in the classics and mathematics under Dr. Finley must have excited in her the warmest feelings of respect, such attainments being out of the reach of women. There may be those to cry out that I claim much for my character at so early a period of my career, but it is not I who originate the claim.

I had the heartiest assurance of my mother and other females of my family that these things were so, and, since they have always shown themselves to be persons of great judgment and verity, I can do no less than to accept their opinion, hoping that, if there be any immodesty in my so doing, it may be attributable to the fondness of their regard.

In respect to my feeling for Miss Gray, I have little leaning to outward appearance as a test of true worth, yet I will never attempt to deny that I found some attraction in the lady's uncommon likeliness of face and form, and in the gracefulness of her bearing. What must account for my graver consideration, however, is the fact that, although exhibiting a taste for frivolity which disturbed me somewhat, I believed her, underneath, to be of an exceedingly serious character. She at all times manifested a ready sympathy with a mind investigating the deeper things of life; she had a quick perception of the beauties of the classics — when translated and pointed out to her—and a suddeness of insight concerning the foibles of those partisans who advocate pernicious liberality in divers questions—when the two sides of the debate had been explained to her.

I have remarked the same quality in all the agreeable women I have ever known. Miss Amelia Robbins is to this day an almost perfect example of it.

But I digress from the sunshiny morning. After greeting me as I joined her, "Where shall we go?" cried Miss Gray.

"Miss Sylvia," I made reply, as she descended the steps from the gate, "it matters little whither we betake ourselves this morning, for—"

"Why?" she interrupted, at the same time casting down her eyes and speaking in a low voice. I remember thinking her manner strange, and it still seems so to me. There were many incomprehensible things about this young lady, as must be luminously set forth ere the conclusion of my narrative.

"Because," I said, briskly, "to him who possesses a true understanding of the art of conversation, time and place count for little."

"Then why should we walk at all?" she asked.

"Why, indeed?" said I, pausing; but straightway she went on, even quickening her steps instead of stopping; so, without more ado, I followed.

"Shall we go to the brook, Mr. Sudgeberry?" she asked, as we reached the lane. "Shall we cross the fields?" Not waiting for my assent, she climbed the stile, and we set off toward the brook.

"How glorious it is to be stirring so early!" says she, presently. "See the dew shining on the cobwebs in the grass, and hark to the birds in the grove. La! I could dance for the very gayety of it!" And she began to sing a little song.

It had ever been my custom to reply to such outbursts of Miss Gray's with some thoughtful sentiment, delivered in a serious tone, as tending to check (or moderate) the ebulliencies of her disposition, hence I answered, walking the while with quiet dignity:

"How often do we unthinkingly pass by lessons which humble nature sets forth for our improvement! Here in the lowly cobweb we see an allegory, if we be not too heedless. What lesson do you obtain from it, Miss Gray?"

My purpose was effected at once, for the song, which was an idle one, with no moral to it, ceased, and she became all interest and sympathy.

"What lesson, Mr. Sudgeberry?" she inquired, gravely.

"Why," I answered, "the lesson of industry, of perseverance!"

"Yes, indeed, Mr. Sudgeberry. I see; the spider's industry. How appropriate!"

I looked upon her approvingly, and continued:

"See how laboriously he has builded himself a place of refuge and rest for his weary head, a retreat where he may raise and shelter his young, and—"

"Surely," she interrupted, "I have read somewhere that the females do that."

Quite confounded for the moment, I walked on in silence, whereupon she began to sing again. Then, not because the sound of her voice was distasteful to me (although I have no great patience with music of any sort), but because I regarded the theme of the song as unworthy to occupy time which might be spent in profitable interchange of ideas, I began a modest dissertation upon the place allegory has occupied in history. "Oh," I concluded, "how easily it puts to shame the baser uses of fiction! How unworthy the time thrown away upon the study of poetry — except the classics — compared to that which is enriched by the reading of allegories, great moral truths tending ever to our improvement in diligence and learning, and conceived by the loftiest intellects for our advancement and profit!"

Our walk had fatigued Miss Gray, for at

this moment she exclaimed, with an accent of relief: "How beautiful, Mr. Sudgeberry! Here we are at the brook," and sat down in the grass.

After ascertaining that the ground was not damp, the sun having by this time sucked up all the dew, I sat down beside her. We were upon a knoll which ran down to the little stream, and, shaded by a group of great trees, our position was not unpleasant. The spot was remote from the customary haunts of the youth of the neighborhood, a fact upon which I considered us both subject for felicitation, the more so because we appeared to have escaped the attendance of an intolerable fellow, William Fentriss, who was everlastingly lolling at or near the Grays' domicile. Indeed, I had been under some apprehension that he might spy us as we crossed the fields, and join us, forcing upon us his idle talk, which had no capacity to be aught but the veriest nonsense, utterly unintelligible to an intellect concerned with anything of weight or worth.

This impertinent, though never my companion, was my fellow-student at Nassau Hall, being one year beneath me; and in that I could treat him with the superiority I felt. He was much about taverns, fretted when a horse fell sick, loved dogs, music, and the new poets; and at Princeton lavished those golden hours of youth in wanton idling or profitless visiting with the liveliest young ladies of the surrounding country. Nor could I understand how he was tolerated by women of tone, refinement, or cultivation, being, as he was, always grossly overdressed to the extreme point of every changing fashion; but even the most impeccable model of female decorum and charm called this rattle "*fascinating*"(!) "*handsome*"(!) and, to my amazement, proved ready with a gracious smile whenever he came near.

It was impossible to comprehend how Miss Gray could find his conversation worth hearing, or how she could permit his continued presence near her; and I judged the present time to be appropriate for the venturing of a few remarks which might indicate, indirectly and delicately, her error, and at the same time point out the preferable merits of true worth as subject for her esteem. I did not wish to make her very unhappy, yet I hoped for a few signs of contrition.

Therefore, after turning over the matter in my mind and thinking up with care the opening sentences, as well as the general trend of the conversation as it should be directed, I began as follows:

"Oh, how oft," said I—for I felt there could be no harm in a somewhat poetical phrase or two—"how oft in the lot of man does he encounter circumstances and things which leave him speechless with amazement, upon which there is no profit in pondering, and as a final dictum upon which there can be no other than the simple words, 'I do not understand!' "

"There can be no doubt of that," agreed Miss Gray, looking thoughtfully at the buckle of my shoe.

"Take, as an instance," I continued, "an

anomaly furnished by human nature. How frequently do we see true merit neglected, or even despised, for the sake of those more gaudy allurements which lie but upon the surface! If it were given to me to consult an oracle (I have explained to you this usage of the ancients, I think), there is one question I would propound to it before any other, and that is: 'Why do ladies sometimes prefer the idle and superficial to those from whom they might derive lasting benefits of a serious and learned nature?' A spectacle I have sometimes observed, one which has astonished me beyond all others, is that of young females, apparently sane and desirous of improvement, listening with seeming pleasure to the conversation of the light and sprightly—ay! to all appearances *enjoying* the society of mere men of fashion, who pour into their ears pernicious extravagances, pitiful nonsensicalities, and flippant nothings, while philosophical, studious, and pious youths who are incapable of lightness, and who would scorn to utter a word unfraught with earnest sobriety or profoundest learning, are allowed to remain unnoticed!"

Here, I judged, the tone of my expressions demanded more than ordinary address; so, with proper gravity and deliberation, I reached out to take her hand, which lay close to mine upon the grass; but, encountering a spider-nest in my progress toward it, the mother-spider issued from the interior of her mansion and bit me on the thumb, which I was forced to place in my mouth in order to extract her poison. Nevertheless, it could be discerned that my argument had not been without its effect upon Miss Sylvia, for she cast down her eyes and turned her face away.

"Let us now consider," I was beginning to continue, approaching my climax—when we suffered an interruption of the most annoying description.

From a group of trees on our right came the sounds of a guitar, strummed in preliminary chords, and then a man's voice, the airy, impertinent quality of which I was at no loss to recognize, though the singer was hidden from our sight, buzzed out the following ditty, to which we were compelled to listen willy-nilly:

"When Beauty wanders far from home
For a June-time ramble,
Then Cupid starts to ambush her
At a rapid amble.

"Sylvia, Sylvia, turn not away;
Hark to the words I'd be saying.
Sylvia, Sylvia, Love lurks all day
Where'er your feet go a-straying!

"No fancy could depict what charms
Always must surround her,
Till Cupid heralds them abroad
When he's caught and bound her.

"Sylvia, Sylvia, never berate!
List to the song I'd be sighing.
Sylvia, Sylvia, Love lies in wait,
Ever his nets for you trying."

"So!" I exclaimed, with great contempt, at the conclusion. "What vain pretension to elegance is disclosed in the imperfections of the last stanza! One does not 'sigh' a song, but sings it. 'Tis pulled in with a rope for the rhyme!"

At this moment William Fentriss stepped into view from behind the trunk of a great tree, and, the guitar swung over his shoulder by a silken ribbon, came toward us with the easy swagger and confident manner of which true impudence is invariably master. Such cheerful insolence, combined with greater foppery of attire, mine eyes have never beheld.

"Nay, nay!" cries he. "A song to cruel Lady Sylvia must needs be sighed. Take my word, Mr. Sudgeberry, 'tis the only way to find half their favor. Sigh, sir, be humility itself, and you will win half of a lady's heart."

"And the other half, Mr. Fentriss?" smiled Miss Gray. I could not understand her smiling, after what I had said to her.

"Oh, for the other half, you'd best take a stick and beat her," he answered, laughing. "But, until you have won the first portion, constantly prostrate yourself at her feet."

With that he deliberately flung himself on the ground within an inch of Miss Gray's shoes, and marvellous clumsy I thought he looked.

"And sigh," says he. And he fetches a sigh. Never have I seen an uninvited person appear more invited.

After a pause, "Such gayety, Mr. Sudgeberry!" says he. At this I showed the scorn I felt by so stern and commanding a frown that he had surely been confounded and left in pitiable consternation, but Miss Gray intervened.

"What a pretty day!" she instantly exclaimed.

"*In*deed," I was replying, "it—"

I achieved only so far when the impudent varlet took the words out of my mouth, as though the lady's remark were addressed to him.

"A morning of the gods!" he cried. "A perfect day, no sweeter ever dawned. Pearls and emeralds under foot, amethystine clouds on sapphire overhead — a jewel of a day! What wonder nymphs stroll abroad! I leave it to Mr. Sudgeberry if a woman is a woman on such a morning. The poorest of the sex becomes a divinity in these airs. And what does the fairest appear"—with a look at Miss Gray which methought must have near made her buffet him—"when the meanest of her sisters is so transfigured? Queen Titania herself, faith!"

"In that case, sir," I said, loftily, "she has small use for flatterers and idlers; queens, if they have been brought up properly, discovering early in life how to detect such gentry. Queens, sir," I repeated with dignity, "queens, having sober lessons to learn, far prefer employment in useful and improving conversations with persons of sense and breeding. Queen Titania, rest assured, would have small interest in the cheap figure of speech which would turn nature into a goldsmith's shop."

"No," said he; "you would have her still

in love with the gentleman with the ass's head!" And he burst into a mannerless guffaw.

Here Miss Gray rose in haste, and announced that she must be returning, as the sun would soon be too warm for pleasure on the homeward stroll. I marked with indignation that our unwelcome companion proposed to accompany us, and this purpose he had the effrontery to carry out, I walking in intense and biting silence, he chattering as easily as though he had not thoroughly disgraced his bringing-up in a dozen ways, while he made such speeches to the lady as I thought must have undoubtedly called forth a chilling rebuke; but none came, to my sore regret.

When we reached her gate, Miss Sylvia turned and bade us good-morning, with a little nod to each.

"Such a pleasant stroll you've given me!"

"Yes," I replied, "*to* the brook."

"Was it not!" said William. "I was but

a little way behind you. The walk *from* the brook has been too warm for you, Mr. Sudgeberry? We must go again."

"We!" I exclaimed. "*We!*"

"Good-morning, gentlemen!" cried Miss Gray, and she ran into the house.

THE CONFESSION OF LOVE

THE events I have described may be accepted as a sample of what took place throughout the summer. Time and again, I would no sooner have Miss Gray's company to myself and open an instructive conversation, or begin the deduction of some truth for her benefit, than that graceless fellow would pop up and hurl his nonsensicalities upon us. Nor can it be denied that he often succeeded in cutting me off from her attention almost entirely by drawing her away into obscure recesses, when I seldom failed to be thrown into the society of her father, a stout, dull old gentleman, who appeared to have no more profit or capacity for improvement in him than a pulpy oyster.

Nothing could have been clearer than that Mr. Fentriss's assiduities often annoyed Miss Sylvia, but he never would have believed it, so conceited is impudence, so secure in its own fastness. Even a well-merited rebuke which he had from her failed to shake him. Tossing up her head at some brazen love-making (he made love to her under my very eyes), she turned pointedly to me, one evening, while I was endeavoring to converse with old Mr. Gray, and said:

"Please talk to me in an improving way, Mr. Sudgeberry. No, Mr. Fentriss, I prefer listening to something profound. I'll hear no more of the speeches you make during the winter and use again upon us poor home ladies in summer. Proceed, Mr. Sudgeberry; I am all ears. Let me have some great lesson, please."

I at once began a conversation on the decline and fall of the Persian Empire, to which she listened attentively, while I triumphantly watched my rival, yet looked in vain to see him betray signs of defeat and shame. Had *I* suffered the public rebuke which he had so well merited and received, I should have hung my head and left the place, but he was without the power to perceive his own downfall.

Evening after evening, on repairing to Miss Gray's, I found him already there—always before me, even when I arrived hours before sunset. This almost led me to suppose that Miss Sylvia might be in the habit of asking him to dine with her and her father, but I dismissed the suspicion as unworthy, with the conclusion that, if he did dine with them, it was because he forced himself upon them. He was capable of it.

Another thing to his discredit: while the mere fact of his preceding me in arrival at the Grays' should have dictated to him an early departure, he was so insensate that he always managed to remain until after I had left—this, too, in spite of many a strong hint from both the young lady and myself, and also in spite of the circumstance that I stayed there every night till I could fairly hold up my head no longer, and was forced to depart through sheer drowsiness at a time long after decent folk had gone to bed. I say I sometimes hinted at this in his presence; so did Miss Gray; and as for old Mr. Gray, he openly said it, along toward midnight. I have even known the latter to groan without disguise, and most piteously; but what effect did that have on William Fentriss? None in the wide world! Did he budge from his chair? Not he! So impervious was he that he would brazenly reply to the good old man with the mockery of a responsive sigh. No comment on such conduct is necessary.

Hour after hour would we sit, watching for each other to go, he ensconced nearer Miss Sylvia—his art in accomplishing this feat was little short of magic—and I would have to

"HOUR AFTER HOUR WE WOULD SIT"

converse with old Mr. Gray. I often raised my voice in order that the lady might have the benefit of my remarks, but at such times Fentriss would break into peals of laughter over some private witticism of his own (I made sure) and my effect would be lost.

Often I thought I should die of the effort of talking to that dull old man. When I would come to a climax in my discourse, and, striking the main question of a theme, thus, perhaps, putting it—"And what, then, *was* this all-pervading error of the ancients?"—I would give, of course, the proper rhetorical pause, intending to proceed at once; but invariably old Mr. Gray would appear to think I had finished the subject, and immediately interject some such remark as, "The north field is looking very well for oats."

Can any intelligent mind require me to enlarge upon the mere statement that the introduction of such observations into the heart of a discussion leaves its logical continuance wellnigh impossible, and must ever be the occasion of acute distress to any earnest expounder?

Mr. Fentriss continued to take up so much of Miss Sylvia's time that perhaps I might have been brought at last to suspect it was by her connivance, except for some expressions of hers which fell to my knowledge by a happy chance.

The evening before the occurrence I mention, I had made (to Mr. Gray) a long and able defence of infant damnation, tracing the doctrine and quoting many commentators with laborious exactitude. Now, I would not have it thought that my efforts went always in vain, or were expended entirely without result upon my constant listener. Nay, the influence I came gradually to exert over him is another proof to me that determined perseverance *cannot* go unrewarded. May I confess it was not without a degree of pleasure that, as time went on, I perceived my conversation producing, little by little, a stronger and stronger effect upon Miss Sylvia's father?

I have known him to be so moved by my modest flights that, at the end, he would reply thickly, even (I may say) with a broken utterance. What suitor, let me ask, is not glad of a power obtained over the near relatives of the admired one? And was not my pride pardonable for this achievement, which, as the sequel shows, I had performed entirely by means of my own unaided conversation? Therefore, I shall make no apology for recording my triumphs in that direction.

This evening Mr. Gray appeared somewhat restless during my argument, but the peroration fixed him in his chair as immovable as if I had pinned him to it with a knife. I made sure that I had thoroughly convinced him, and was confirmed in this impression when he rose and explained, with a curious incoherency in his voice, that he must consult some of the authorities in his library; but he did not return, though I waited a considerable time.

The following afternoon I was riding along

a quiet lane, with the reins on old Jeremiah's neck, and perusing a work of merit, when, glancing up, I chanced upon the pleasant discovery of two mounted figures some distance ahead of me, which I recognized as those of Miss Gray and her father. I clapped my book in my pocket and quickened my nag's gait to overtake them, but as I drew near I perceived they had not noticed my approach, the dust being thick and muffling the hoof-beats, so I pulled in, meaning to come upon them unexpectedly and give them a pleasant surprise. Thus, by chance, I happened to overhear part of their conversation.

Mr. Gray appeared to be laboring under no little excitement, flinging his arms about in the most vigorous gestures. It was a warm afternoon, and that part of the back of his neck unprotected by his queue was quite purple.

"Saints and martyrs!" cries the profane old man with singular vehemence. "I'll bear it no longer! I will not! Do you want to see your old father in a mad-house? For the sake of my white hairs tell that fool to go away and stay there!"

At this my heart beat high with happiness. "Aha!" thinks I, "I was right: my work has not gone in vain; Mr. Gray is on my side. Now, Master Will, I wish you had been here to hear her father's opinion of you."

It was not difficult to see that Miss Sylvia was amused. "Stop your laughing!" the old gentleman bawled, violently. "It's no laughing matter. I've fallen off three stone this summer, and I'd rather take the plague than go through it again. You've got to let me talk to Fentriss."

"So!" thought I, my respect for Mr. Gray vastly increased, "Master Will is not to bother me much longer. This good old man will send him about his business a-humming."

"Why do you let him come?" the old gentleman asked, angrily.

"To amuse you, father dear," responded the daughter, roguishly.

"Amuse me!" I feared Mr. Gray would

burst his coat seams. "If you are going to have the other, why—"

Here, with joy, I saw the fair one bend her head in maiden modesty, while her voice fell so low I scarce could hear the words she said. Her posture, graceful and coy, bespoke a sudden shyness, as tender as it was, in her, unexpected—an attitude of revelation which, I confess, caused a thrill, a warmth of satisfaction to pass through my veins. I admit, additionally, that for some inexplicable reason both the thrill and the satisfaction were irrationally increased by the manner in which, as she began to blush exceedingly, the wave of her hair, falling from her brow, shone against the gentle crimson of that brow and of her cheek.

She turned her downcast eyes away from her father, so that her profile was toward me; then she lifted her face and her glance, and spoke—to the air, it seemed.

"You know—ah, do I need to say it?—there is only one in the whole world that I—"

She paused.

I would listen no more to a confession so much to my advantage, and therefore, coughing loudly, I gave my nag a flick and rode up beside them.

Judge the pleasure of my feelings when I saw that my arrival threw the object of my affections into the most delightful, the most overwhelming confusion. At the same time, good Mr. Gray, in his surprise, welcomed me with broken monosyllables and cries of pleased amazement.

It must be plain to all that it now remained for me to choose when I should put the question. Secure in her father's approval, aware of my place in her own good graces, and knowing their joint condemnation of my rival, I was privileged to laugh in my sleeve, after this, when the unconscious Fentriss would talk all evening to Miss Gray, leaving me to address myself diligently to her good father.

At this period I had fears that all was not well with Mr. Gray's constitution, and I believe that he was having business troubles, for he sometimes suffered spells of terrible depression; also, his complexion took on a sickly, pallid hue, unusual and sinister in a full-blooded person.

THE TOAST

ONLY one thing could have added to my triumph and the pleasure of it; and that very thing was the actual accomplishment of the next week, whereby William Fentriss was exhibited in his true character, left outside the pale of reputable company, and, moreover, through an incident as happy for us as unfortuitous for him, utterly banished from Mr. Gray's and his daughter's society.

In the city, a few miles distant, there lived —if gyrating to the fiddles all night and snoring abed all day be living—a number of romping, Mohawkish youths who were friends of William Fentriss. One Saturday night—well I recall it, for was it not the first evening of the summer he did not obtrude himself upon Miss Sylvia and me?—Will repaired to town for a banquet given by these roisterers. Now, emerging from their feast, befuddled and enervated by the noxious fumes of their potations, the party rioted confusedly over the place till the watch was summoned; the young men were surrounded, and, in the state of enfeeblement which had befallen them, easily captured and conveyed to the lock-up.

Such exploits, vicious as they should always be considered, were too commonly overlooked in those days; but our community was, for the greater part, a proper, serious, disciplinarian one; so that by noon the next day Will Fentriss was being held up as a warning example to every apple-thieving or anywise-depraved child of the whole country-side, for the story was immediately brought out to us and widely spread; and, though there were found those impertinent enough to offer excuse for the young man, alleging in defence his early departure from the banquet, before the acts of maraudery were committed, yet none could deny he had been of the party, or that the dissolute young men were his friends; therefore sentiment was justly strong against him.

There was one curious detail connected with his actions which I shall not overlook, but which has received more weight in the minds of many than its due; indeed, there have been people dull enough to use it as the basis of a completely laughable theory concerning Miss Gray's course in regard to William—a theory so far from being borne out by the facts that I need not more definitely mention it. The origin of this nonsense was the report that at the banquet, when the toasts to the ladies were called, and William's turn came, he rose, and instead of crying "I give you Sylvia!" as all expected, pronounced the name "Cherry!"

Now, as our neighborhood was the abode of no person of this appellation, nor were any of the gossips acquainted with such elsewhere, the very next morning there was a clacking about the matter which bade fair to outdo and smother the righteous indignation over Will's wildness and perpetrations; there was also a vast curiosity and a hopeful prying concerning the identity of Miss Cherry, with much wondering how Sylvia Gray would take it. This, of course, was the very arrogance of misconception; as well I knew, since the day I rode up behind Mr. Gray and Miss Gray, that William Fentriss might toast a thousand Cherrys if he would, it was less than nothing to Sylvia.

About two of the afternoon, I think it may have been, as I sat engaged with my studies beneath an apple-tree, near our front gate, I heard my name called—somewhat tremulously—from the road, and, turning, beheld Miss Gray herself upon her little bay mare.

She impatiently awaited my approach, flicking her skirt with her whip and glancing up and down the road. I could not fail to perceive her very visible agitation, nor did I find the expression of her emotions unbecoming. Her eyes, now veiled as she followed the flickings of her whip-lash, now turning away from me, then toward me, but never directly meeting mine, were of a troubled brightness; her breath came quick; her face was overspread with a high color; her whole attitude betokened excited determination.

"Saddle your horse, Mr. Sudgeberry," says she. "I wish you to ride with me, if you please."

Then well I understood that flushing brow, that heaving bosom, that tumultuous yet decided glance. Having cognizance of the condition of her affections, here was no trying riddle to read. I was convinced that she was as lady-like and proper a maiden as breathed, and who could have conceived more readily than I that conflict with pride, ere she allowed herself to come seeking a gentleman's society, instead of waiting at home for his invitations?

When I stood beside her, she looked over my head for a moment, with a great sweetness, before speaking.

"I was engaged to walk at this hour with Mr. Fentriss. I prefer to ride with you." She finished, faltering tenderly, "That is, if you—if you wish."

At this point I came near making a declaration of my purposes regarding her future. However, I had already given the question a searching consideration, deciding not to speak until the Christmas holidays, and my wisdom now held me silent; for a betrothal, at the present time, entailing a reciprocal correspondence when I returned to Nassau Hall, would have interfered with my studies during the following term, which was the crucial one of the whole course. In truth, had I not thus with a stern hand regulated my conduct, I might have lost the Latin prize, the apex and climax of my career as a student.

I replied to Miss Sylvia's request cautiously, making reference to my scholarly tasks for the afternoon with a regretful glance at my books, as I judged it expedient in dealing with a woman, plainly to exhibit the sacrifices made for her; yet, practising a subtlety at once innocent and dexterous, I gave her at the same time to understand that I was far from unwilling to fall in with her invitation.

In less than half an hour we were jogging side by side along the road, she leaning toward me from her saddle with the most blushing and flattering attention to my discourse. Never had man a more perfect listener than I that afternoon. Her orbs of vision, exponents of the enrapt mind, were fixed upon the distance; in them dwelt a profound glow which gratified me exceedingly; and the people whom we met turned and stared after us as we went by. This, also, was a source of pleasure.

But nothing touched me to such extreme delight that day as the first sight of Will Fentriss's face when he saw us riding up the road together.

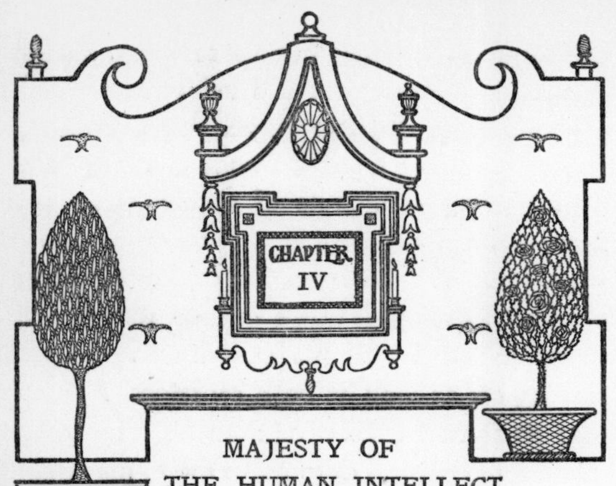

MAJESTY OF THE HUMAN INTELLECT

ONE fine evening near the close of the following week, Mr. Gray, Miss Sylvia, and I sat upon the veranda in sympathetic converse, when whom should we behold, walking toward us from the gate in the clear moonlight, but old Vawter Fentriss, Will's uncle and guardian.

Vawter Fentriss was a loose, apple-cheeked old man, full of hoarse jests—a shame to his years. You could not pass his house any day in good weather but to see him, always dressed in a green coat and velvet cap, romping among his dogs, or mayhap seated on the rim of the horse-trough, smoking a long pipe, an admiring semicircle of stable-boys and farm-servants listening to Heaven knows what kind of tales from his undignified lips. He would exchange quips in loud shouts with every passer-by of his acquaintance, never leaving off as long as both remained in hearing; so that the sober-minded were forced to make long, painful détours to avoid his house.

However, the dullest might have remarked that it was with no jocular intent he adventured to-night's visit; his heavy face was troubled and anxious, while ever and anon he kicked at some of the hounds that had followed him.

I observed Miss Sylvia's demeanor with commendation and approval. She rose as if to greet the visitor, but, vouchsafing only a word, held herself haughtily, and, returning Vawter's salutations with a proud bearing, showed him a chair by Mr. Gray.

"Nay," says he, "I'll not sit, thank you. I am here on an errand to you, Miss Sylvia, and—" He came to a halt, as though hoping she might offer to speak with him in private. Therein disappointment was his meed, for she, at once taking on a patient languor, looked over his head with the air of one kept waiting for a very indifferent pleasure.

At this he showed considerable discomfort, knowing not how to continue. "Well," he observed, presently, "it is a fine night. I just thought I would come by this way." There was no reply, and after a silence of some duration he wiped his face several times with his kerchief, and repeated, in a low voice, "I just thought I would come by this way." Then he kicked a couple of his dogs down the steps, apologizing for their presence, as nothing could withhold them from following him wherever he went. That done, he stood muttering that it was a fine night, until one of the dogs again obtruded himself upon the steps, whereat his master turned and booted him clean over another dog. This seemed of great benefit to Mr. Fentriss.

"Hey!" he shouted, his tongue suddenly loosened. "Am I to stand here like a frozen ninny and have even the manners of my own dogs disgrace me? Will you tell me," he continued, turning upon Mr. Gray, with an expression amazingly choleric, "what it is you have against my boy?"

"*I!*" exclaimed Mr. Gray. "What have *I* done against him?"

"Will's a good lad," cried Vawter—"as good and well-behaved as any living—yet here, because of a little gayety, and the granny-patter over it, you forbid him your house. What kind of neighborliness do you say that is?"

"*I* forbid him the house!" said the other. "I had nothing to do with it. I—"

"Why, it is common talk all over the place that he was forbidden to come here, that you disapproved his courses, that—"

"I tell you, sir," interrupted Mr. Gray, "I did not forbid him. I had noth—"

But Vawter, in his turn, took the words out of his neighbor's mouth. "Well, Heaven pardon you! Lord-a-mercy! isn't it the common gossip? Will himself could not deny it when I put it to him flat. 'Twas the very day after that supper doings in town. Will was to walk with Miss Sylvia here; she had promised him, but, instead—instead of keeping her word with him, she came riding by with Sudgeberry, just as poor Will came out of your gate, having found her away. Weren't there no others that saw it? Don't tell *me!* I know whereof I speak, Mr. Gray! She wouldn't answer my nephew's bow, and tried to pass him by, making much of Sudgeberry the while; but Will would not have it, and ran in front of her horse. She bade him clear the path, and, upon his begging some explanation, told him, shrewishly, that he had friends in town he'd best return to; that neither she nor you desired more of his company; he was too gay a gentleman, she said; and she gave him the message from you that he was forbid the house — that he was forbid the house!

Wasn't that your message? Hey, sir, if you call that—"

"Now, now!" Mr. Gray cut in. "'Twas only at Sylvia's bidding. She had the tale that Will was in disgrace, and she desired my authority. It may be true I sent some such message, since she wished it, but—"

"Well, what d'ye call that?" said Vawter. "If that ain't forbidding a man your house!"

"'Tis easy to see," Mr. Gray observed, plaintively, "that you have no daughter."

"But I have a nephew."

Mr. Gray lifted his hands in a feeble gesture of protest. "I give it up," he murmured. "I can't make head nor tail of it. What with the evenings I've had and the troubles I've been through this season, what with losing sleep and Sylvia's crying about the house all week, and neighbors quarrelling with me, account of her affairs, I doubt I last the summer."

"You may be troubled," rejoined Vawter, "but so am I. I can't bear to look at Will as he's been since Miss Sylvia has thrown him aside—and for Sudgeberry, here—for do it she did; yes, like an old, moth-eaten cap! D'ye think it's no trouble for me to see the lad sitting the day long in one place with his head in his hands, he that has all his life been the gayest of the gay and made my widower's house cheery, and—" He coughed several times at this point, then spoke up, sharply: "Look, now! Don't think I come from him, or that he knows it. He's proud as you are, ma'am—you might be aware of that—and if you can't be kind to him again, I don't know what we are to do, not for the life o' me! I don't mean he will be doing what is wicked or desperate—he has his good sense, and much of it—but isn't there no word I could say to turn you to him? If there is, I could go on my old knees to you to beg the knowledge of it. Surely you don't need my telling to know that Will's thought the world and all of you, and dreamed of little else these five years. If it is as I hear, and you're angry with him for that toast to

'Cherry,' why, it may be that could be explained."

"*Explained!*"

Sylvia's voice was husky with indignation, and she lifted her head proudly. "He may toast as many 'Cherrys' as he pleases, so he does not come near me. What can it be to me whom he toasts? He is proud, is he? Well, sir, you may tell him that I am too proud myself to allow young men to be the associates of Mohawks and Heaven knows whom, in town, and then seek company in me. He will not sit with his head in his hands long; never you fear for that, sir! 'Twill be a mighty little time till he finds consolation in his 'Cherrys'; and *they* will not be too proud, you will see! — ladies whose names he was free to mention in that society! Proud! 'Tis my one satisfaction, tell him, that he is—or pretends to be—since it keeps him out of my sight."

Now I ask all the world: What completer proof was ever offered that a woman cared nothing for a particular man than this speech of Sylvia's, openly and voluntarily setting forth that Will Fentriss was not, and never could be, the weight of her little finger to her?

Also, observe that Mr. Gray spoke of her weeping much of late. Ay, though I had not seen her weep, I knew she had been dismal enough; and so had I myself, at times; I confess it. The end of my holiday was fast approaching, and with it a separation of months was coming upon us. What wonder that I sighed sometimes—what wonder that she wept?

When she had said her say to Vawter, she turned haughtily and swept away to the other end of the veranda, where she remained, lost in her reflections.

It appeared to me befitting and proper that a few words be hereupon addressed to Mr. Fentriss. Advancing, therefore, to where he stood gasping with astonishment on the steps, I extended the first finger of my right hand toward him in dignified reproof, and exclaimed:

"Oh, sir, fie!"

An expression of the most astounding and immoderate rage suddenly overspread his features.

"Well, upon my soul and vitals!" he burst forth. "If it's come to this, I'll—"

But I cut him off sharply and allowed him not one syllable more.

"Ay, sir!" I cried, loudly. "I repeat: Fie! Fie!—and be ashamed! Compose yourself to a more respectable frame of mind, and your visage to a seemlier aspect, while I expound your own case for your benefit and good. Is it the part of age to be the messenger of petulant youth, justly rebuked and sulking?"

"I'll not stand this!" Vawter replied, in tones which alternated between hoarse remonstrance and apoplectic choking. "If I do, may I—"

I immediately asserted my human right to speech, conquering him by the force and, may I say, the majesty of will-power, which

I possessed to as great a degree in my younger days as now. I poured forth upon him not the phials of contempt, but the silver decanters of eloquent instruction. I gave utterance to the wisdom of the ancients upon the proper paths of conduct for aged men to follow, adding thereunto my own deductions, with an indubitable demonstration that the only course now open to him was a silent and contrite withdrawal.

At first he waved his hands violently, and attempted to drown my words by sundry roarings, near profane, but these gave place to a dangerous coughing fit, so that he was forced to pound himself upon the chest, after which an awed silence fell upon him; for it may be here recorded that an inspiration—nothing less—sustained my flow of thought upon this occasion. Never in my life have I been more fluent.

As I went on, he slowly backed himself down the steps, until, as he came into the moonlight, no one could have failed to perceive that consternation alone was writ upon his face. His little red eyes were opened to an extent no man ever saw before or again. I followed him, whereat he faintly motioned at me with the palm of his hand held outward, as if to keep me off, and retreated toward the gate.

At last we had the satisfaction of seeing his discomfiture complete. He went rapidly down the lane in the moonlight, his chin on his chest, a crushed and humbled man, his dogs slinking after him, not bounding and barking as they had arrived, but bearing their tails concavely on the inner curve. As for myself, I sank, somewhat exhausted, but triumphant, upon the steps.

There is but one thing more to tell of Vawter Fentriss. As I have recounted, it was his daily habit to sit somewhere about his grounds and exchange quips with all who passed his house, shouting gibes and jests at every passer-by of his acquaintance until out of hearing, and I had not escaped his feeble wit whenever I went that way. Now let me chronicle the result of this night's address to him: I write it simply, and without parade or pride; but from that time forth he called not another jest at me to the day of his death; and I never afterwards passed his house that he did not get up from his seat, or quit whatever he was doing, and go into the house as soon as he caught sight of me.

The man had some shame.

THE NOTE

ONLY a week now intervened before my departure, and while the thought of this would naturally cast a dark shadow over the spirits of my friends, causing in them a plainly apparent though silent depression, still that was a truly delightful period; for the mar-pleasure, William Fentriss, was absent, nor during several days did one of us catch the slightest glimpse of his outrivalled and disgraced head.

Each evening, at earliest dusk, I repaired to the house of my mistress, cogitating and formulating by the way, so that the time, though pleasant, should be spent in improvement and to the profit of all three of us—for Mr. Gray still made one of our little party. Many and many a time did he, out of delicacy, arise and make as if he were about to withdraw, but, in spite of a thousand earnest excuses and protestations which he offered, Miss Sylvia ever firmly detained him, being a conscientious daughter, who would not alone enjoy a pleasure or a benefit when she could possibly share it with those to whom her duty lay.

On that account I still directed toward the old man a great part of my conversation. To do otherwise, I maintain, would have been a graceless act. He had been my nightly companion and constant listener throughout the whole season. Should I desert him now? Such a treachery it was not in my nature to conceive.

Miss Sylvia, as I have indicated, was possessed by a melancholy which grew deeper each day, betrayed by the saddening of her features, those sorrowful images of her emotions; but as for myself, I was conscious of a warmish tingle of excitement; the highest spirits followed my triumph; seldom, indeed, have I been more joyously inclined, and at any time could I have talked till daylight. This pleasurable agitation took the place of rest, and thus, feeling no need of sleep, I was enabled to make my calls at the Grays' extend far into the night.

In my enthusiasm I selected only the gravest topics, often, I fear, going too deep for Mr. Gray to follow. Let that be as it may, I can truthfully declare that it became an actual pleasure to talk to him. I have not the wish to assume undue credit, yet it was no unworthy performance to arrest his attention and restrain him from brooding upon the business troubles which I have mentioned. To this end I exerted every endeavor; I called into play my utmost powers, as I saw the inroads his anxieties had made upon his hitherto hardy constitution. His hands were nerveless; his flesh had grown flabby; a dull, fishy glaze was come over his eyes, together with a perpetual twitching of the lids which would have softened a heart of adamant.

He was far from being the man he had been at the first of that summer, not only physically, but mentally; for there were times when the glaze would leave his eyes, and I could see them shining in the darkness with a baleful light, like the eyes of a beast at bay. Simultaneously his sunken lips would work and mumble, and he would whisper and hiss to himself, so that I feared for his reason.

When these unhappy spells came over him I would fare on briskly with whatever discussion was in hand, pretending I noticed nothing. So, presently, his head would fall on his chest, and I comprehended—without his saying it—that he was grateful to me for soothing him. It is the unspoken gratitude which is deepest.

William Fentriss took his departure three days before mine, but he did not do so out of any virtuous anxiety to renew his studies you may be sure. The afternoon before he went, I had the pleasure of passing him in the lane with Miss Sylvia upon my arm. I could not tell whether it was from sheer insolence, or if it was to conceal (which it did not) the extreme, painful flushing of his face, but he ventured a very low, formal bow, receiving in return the cut direct for his pains. We swept on with the finest air, and left him standing there with his head bared. I could not repress a pleasant laugh, in which the lady joined me, though I could feel her arm tremble with anger at his impudence.

This indignation of hers was not suffered to diminish, for, on returning from our stroll, a note was brought to her, which she opened and read in my presence, her face growing even redder than Will's had been. Her hand, as she did so, again shook with rage, a passion, in this instance, appreciably enhancing the youthful charms appertaining to her appearance.

"Read it," she said, furiously, thrusting the paper upon me. "Read it, sir! Read it, for it is you whom I ask to carry the answer, which is this scrawl, back to him again. Does he think that I shall bear everything?"

The note was short. I read it.

"Adieu madam, I have just now determined to go away upon the morrow. You have put a great deal of shame upon me, and for nothing. Yet, let me tell you, I have only thanks for your former kindness. You and your escort had the enjoyment of laughing at me a little while ago. Believe me, your choice of another to favor causes me the greater mortification—but the lesser alarm.

"You will not speak to me. You will not hear me. You draw your skirts aside lest they touch me as you pass. Yet I shall make you listen, make you speak to me, *gladly*, ere the year be run. Never fear but I shall win you. *Ah, aear Sylvia!*"

I did not carry the note to Will myself. I took it home with me, and sent it to him by a bearer, deciding upon that as the course of greater discretion.

But before I sent it, I sat me down and wrote upon the back of it the following words:

"Opened by Miss Gray—and me—by mistake."

THE FAREWELL

AS I turned in at the gate for my last evening, I observed Mr. Gray get up from the porch and go hastily into the house. "Good old man!" I thought, smiling slightly at this mark of his emotion. "His attachment is indeed sincere!"

Taking possession of the easy-chair he had vacated, I commenced the conversation with Miss Sylvia by addressing her upon the honor due every virtuous and indulgent parent, offering also, in particular, a few hints tributary to Mr. Gray's susceptibilities as well as his thoughtfulness in continuing to remain in-doors (as he did) upon such an occasion; whereat she seemed somewhat cheered.

I had not long continued in this strain when there befell that incident which, while it might have produced an impression almost painful as a betrayal of the pitch to which the supremity of her sentiments had brought her, must remove the last cloud from the minds of any who yet retain a doubt as to the direction in which those sentiments tended.

I was drawing to a close my references to Mr. Gray's emotion and the delicacy of his absence, when the appreciative smile that had lightened her melancholy began to increase with unnatural rapidity; she seized convulsively upon her lace kerchief and covered her face with it. She held it there for several moments, when, suddenly, from beneath the lace rang out a laugh, silvery indeed, yet of such wildness that I jumped to my feet in alarm.

Nor did the bell-like cachinnations cease upon my action; louder and louder they rang, as the fit seized upon her; peal after peal startled the stilly night.

Never before, in all my days, had I heard or seen any person laugh as she did then; never, have I since, one who laughed so distractedly, so uncontrollably; never one in throes so long protracted. She laughed until I feared she might swoon from exhaustion.

She rocked herself to and fro, and back and forth, now clasping her sides, then stretching forth her arms as if for breath, and at last, consumed by the very anguish of laughter, utterly lost to her own command, could only faintly beat the air with her hands.

Thus did the unhappy demon of hysteria enter into her, and although the fit was entirely unlooked-for on my part, I remained not an instant in doubt as to its cause, remembering well upon the eve of what day we stood. Hence I spoke soothingly to her, encouraging her to patience, reminding her that my term of absence would last only a few months, also exhorting her to recall the fact that I had every intention of returning for some days at Christmas-time.

My efforts were of little avail, being greeted by a renewal of the attack, which came on with redoubled force. So, having heard that such disorders might be quelled by distracting the mind of the victim to some interesting topic foreign to the cause of the convulsion, I began a description of the catacombs.

Again I failed to calm her. She cried out some words too indistinct for interpretation, but by her pitiful gesticulations I made out that she desired me to speak no farther upon either subject, and to leave her for a time, while she endeavored to compose herself.

Therefore, I retired to the end of the veranda, where I remained while she arose, and, with feeble steps, paced up and down the path to the gate in the cool starlight. Ever and anon the symptoms of her malady broke out afresh, but the outbursts recurred with less and less violence, until, after the lapse of half an hour, or thereabouts, she was enabled to rejoin me.

She offered some embarrassed apologies; but I spared her maidenly confusion by ordering my bearing as if nothing unusual had occurred, promptly resuming the description of the catacombs where I had left off. This I followed with one of those disquisitions formerly made for Mr. Gray, one which the follies of Fentriss had prevented her from hearing; and it was not long before she was completely restored, and her features resumed their previous aspect of distress.

During the four or five delightful hours that followed — in brief, throughout the remainder of our interview—the signals of her dolor increased, until, knowing that they must be visible, and unable to conceal her agitation, she excused herself and withdrew.

After such an evening who can wonder that I was fearful lest she break down altogether when it came to the farewells of the following afternoon? However, my apprehensions wronged that power of dissimulation, in the presence of third parties, of which her sex so invariably shows itself mistress, and at the final moment she contrived to bear up with surprising fortitude and courage.

But Mr. Gray — that good old man, Mr. Gray! Ah, there was a parting indeed! The tears stood in his eyes; he said "good-bye" a thousand times, murmuring under his breath words which I could not catch, growing more mixed and incoherent every moment, and finally quite giving way to his emotions.

Ah, how wonderfully, little by little, do the seeds of affection grow! Thus, at the beginning of that summer, Mr. Gray and I were nothing to each other. But, drop by drop, I had watered the simple herb of his attachment till it spread and blossomed into a beautiful and wondrous flower. There was not much in common between us; often I felt his mind unable to accompany mine to those higher pinnacles of thought whereunto my own desired to flee, and, after arrival, perch; nor can I say that I ever gave him my whole confidence or friendship; yet the good old man's devotion touched me.

His fingers worked convulsively, so that he had to clinch them tight to hide it. And one of the clearest and most vivid pictures which memory brings of my youth is that which comes before me now, as fresh as though it all happened yesterday: of the good old man (when I turned and looked back from the road) standing there by the steps, his right hand outstretched to wave me farewell, his fingers still clinched to conceal his emotion.

His arm dropped to his side as I turned, and confusion overspread his countenance; for men do not willingly exhibit their deepest feelings. So I left him there in his trouble, with his mouth open.

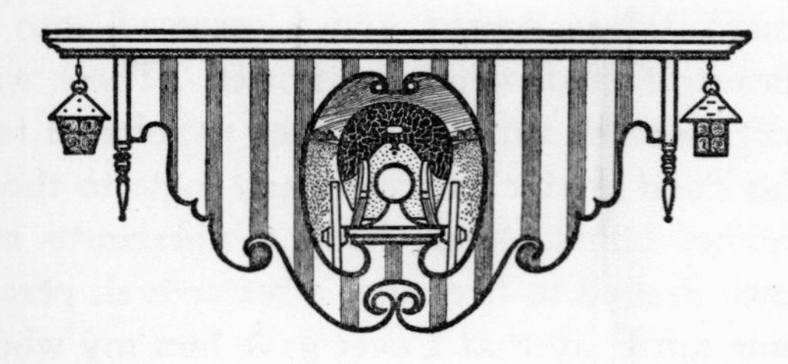

THE INTERVIEW

I FOUND William Fentriss already arrived at Nassau Hall. Although we rarely met, and had little to do with each other, I made out that, so far as his manner in public was an exponent of his condition, his downfall had no improving effect upon him. To all appearances he had recovered every whit of his pristine jauntiness; he was no less impertinent and easy, betraying a consciousness of the disgrace of his wrong-doing by neither those attitudes of shame to which his uncle had alluded nor by visible contrition of the countenance—not he!—nor by moral conduct and a diligent energy at his books. Nevertheless, I learned that he was indifferent to that society he had formerly sought with eagerness in the surrounding country, for now he shunned the ladies, to spend his time dawdling about the country-side on long, lonely rambles, wearing, in spite of the gay exterior he presented in company, a face as long and as lonely as his peregrinations. The demonstration of his true condition, affording ample proof that his gayety covered a secretly gnawing chagrin, was revealed to me through an accident.

On late afternoons, when the bright, declining rays of the sun announced that the day's work was over, and the idler spirits might have been observed playing at toss behind the imposing pile of Nassau, the more dissolute risking the tutor's detection at pitch-the-penny in their chambers, it was my habit to repair to the burying-ground for the purpose of varying my mental activities and preparing my faculties for the night's study by contemplation of the headstones and speculations concerning the eternal punishment of many whose bones reposed beneath.

Seated upon a slab in that soothing spot one pleasant evening, toward twilight, I was occupied in thus recuperating my energies, when my meditations were disturbed by a long-drawn, mournful sigh, of such profundity it almost might have been designated sonorous. The sound, emanating as it did from an unseen source, bore with it, in those surroundings, some measure of alarm, especially as I had believed myself quite solitary. Hence I sat quite still for several moments, while the slab became cold enough to chill my spine, when the sigh fell upon my ears a second time. At that, summoning my temerity, I got to my feet and, moving cautiously, parted some bushes in front of me and peeked through. What was my astonishment to be rewarded by the sight of William, leaning on the fence with an air of complete dejection, his eyes as vacant and troubled as those of a strayed animal.

He retained his dolorous posture for a long time; then, without having been aware of my presence, he departed, sighing as he went, and bending his steps in the direction of Rocky Hill, instead of returning to the village, although it was now the hour for the evening meal and the gloom of dusk was settling down. Often, afterwards, being now on the lookout, I saw him pass that way (always fondly believing himself unobserved), with the same crestfallen and melancholy look, his head bowed on his breast.

The knowledge in this wise afforded me, that his public demeanor was but the mask of a proud trickster, presented me a topic for some not unpleasant reflections. 'Tis well for impudence to realize that, hide as it may under the finest surface, it is no continuing rival for true merit and intelligent attainment.

The term wore on; the holidays were at

hand. It was late of a windy night in December, and I had almost completed my preparations for retiring, when there came a knock at the door. Candle in hand, I drew the bolt, and there, to my astonishment, stood William Fentriss.

I gazed upon him forbiddingly, and inquired his pleasure.

He coolly entered, and, dropping at half-length into my easy-chair, crossed his legs in an attitude of foppish languor, placed the tips of the fingers of his two hands lightly together, and looked at me quaintly, with the faint apparition of a smile in his eyes and on his lips.

"I petition for a word with the master of all learning," he said, assuming a cheerfulness which well I knew he could not feel. "What a charming nightcap you wear! Faith, there'd be conquests a-plenty if you wore it by day! Ah, if only the ladies—"

I interrupted him. "I think the subject of conquests may be a sore one for you in my presence. You exhibit a praiseworthy fortitude in referring to it."

He stared at me a moment. "You give me my just deserts," he rejoined, slowly. "That was well said. We will leave conquests out of our conversation, then, if you please. And may I suggest that you shut the door before you take a cold in that light, though becoming, drapery of yours, Mr. Sudgeberry?"

I took a comfort from my bed, and, folding it round me, at the same time eying him sternly, again requested his business with me.

"I thought it possible that you might consent to my company on the journey home for the holidays," he answered. "I suppose you are going?"

"Certainly, sir," I said.

"If I may make so bold, Mr. Sudgeberry, are you going by coach?"

"No, sir; I shall travel upon the back of a horse my father sends for the purpose."

"Good! You will travel upon the back

of a horse your father sends for the purpose. Now, I live with my uncle, as you may have been so kind as to notice, and my uncle is to send up one of my horses for the same purpose, as regards the back, you observe, that your father designs yours. Well, the roads are vile, the weather is treacherous, and Dr. Finley has ordained that no one, under horrid penalties, may depart until noon of the 24th. Therefore, to reach home for Christmas, we shall be compelled to leave here immediately upon the stroke of twelve; and, the roads and weather being what they are, we stand a chance of riding late into the night, or even of being detained at some way-side tavern until morning. In this, or any case, I offer you my poor company. And also," he continued, with a twinkling glance at me, "we might encounter some gentlemen who would be glad to relieve us of our purses, mayhap cut our invaluable throats. We should add to our safety by making the trip together. Do you think you could bear with me for the dozen hours or so?"

I turned the proposition over in my mind, all my inclinations naturally urging me to return a peremptory and decided refusal. On the other hand, I shrank from the contemplation of the journey, short though it was, in winter, without the assurance of company; and it should be borne in mind that Will and I were the only students who would be going that way. The thought of meeting rough fellows was exceedingly discomforting, the vision of a night attack in the lonely wastes presenting itself to me with horror; while my companion's easy reference to a throat-cutting sent the very chills to my vitals.

I debated the matter carefully, but the considerations I have mentioned finally determined me to close with the offer, though with much reluctance, and I so informed him.

"Splendid! Splendid!" cries he, waving his hand to me. "Splendid, Mr. Sudgeberry! Have your saddle-bags packed and your nag waiting by noon of the 24th, and then, faith! —sola, for home!"

His gayety sprang up suddenly, then as suddenly fell and passed out of him, so that in the same instant he turned a white, tired face upon me, one much older than he had worn in June. He went to the door, bidding me good-night in a melancholy voice:

"Sleep without dreams, Mr. Sudgeberry. Pray for me! 'Nymph, at thine orisons remember—' *Good*-night, sir!"

It was long before I slept that night; not only because William Fentriss's remarks had aroused an uneasiness and fear of misadventure by the way, which insisted upon recurring to my wakeful intellect, loath as I was to dwell upon such a subject, but I feared I had been hasty in my decision, and I was much disturbed to think that I might be seen, perchance by folk from our parts, with this wild, reputationless fellow for my companion.

There was one contingency which I deemed too remote to cause me any anxiety. Mr. Gray and his daughter were in New York, and meant to return—as my advices from home let me know—the day before Christmas. William and I should be several hours ahead of them, and our chance of meeting was so exceedingly slight that, though I had no mind the Grays should see me riding in such company, I dismissed the possibility from my meditations.

I resolved, moreover, that when we came into our own neighborhood I would make some excuse to drop behind and ride separately; and I hoped that whoever might see us together would put the best construction on my conduct, and judge that I accompanied the prodigal in the hope of improving his courses and directing the irregular channels of his mind.

I was the more tranquil because of my assurance that William had no inkling of the information I possessed—that is, of the present whereabouts and intended journey of Mr. Gray and Miss Sylvia. My own family wrote me that it had come to them by accident, and, since the night of Vawter's visit, there had been no communication between the households of Fentriss and Gray. Mr. Gray had gone off suddenly to New York on an errand of business, taking his daughter with him, and setting his return for Christmas Eve.

Deliberating upon these and other matters, and repeating to myself fragments connected with the morrow's scholarly duties, I finally closed mine eyes in profound slumber.

THE JOURNEY

PROMPTLY at noon of the 24th I was cantering down Nassau Street on the good Jeremiah, and looking about for William Fentriss, who was nowhere to be seen. I may state here that my observation seldom has been in fault, and I have often remarked that those who most emphatically impress upon others the necessity for promptitude are most apt themselves to be dilatory. I was internally commenting on this fact with appropriate severity, when I caught sight of Dr. and Mrs. Finley coming up the street, and beside them, chatting merrily, William Fentriss, clad, with his usual worldliness, in a long, white great-coat, open at the throat to show a heavy fall of lace. Beholding me, he waved his hat, and, turning to Mrs. Finley, kissed her hand in farewell with all the outlandish airs of a man of fashion. Nevertheless, the doctor only laughed.

Will mounted a large, black horse, held in waiting at the corner, and, sending a loud view-halloo ringing on the winter air, set his steed in motion to join me; so we presently left the village at a lively gait. Once out on the country road, however, we were forced to pull into a mild canter, and by the time we crossed Stony Brook settled down to a dull jog-trot.

The day was frosty, the sky overcast; rain had fallen all the previous night, but a chill wind, springing up and whistling about our ears uncomfortably, stiffened the mud to that intolerable heaviness through which rapid progress is impossible for the stoutest beast. Presently a thin, damp snow began to fall, and I thought the prospect of reaching our destination that evening blank indeed; certainly we should be upon the road till after nightfall.

These considerations had little effect upon the liveliness of my companion, which had come up in him extraordinarily. He seemed to be in the most cheerful spirits, carolling and singing, and hailing everybody we met with some frivolity or nonsense in regard to Christmas cheer; and especially was this the case when the person happened to be a carter or farmer with a rosy-cheeked lass alongside. At such times William would never leave off calling out compliments till they were fairly out of hearing, while I, inexpressibly mortified, would muffle my face in the cape of my great-coat, hoping to escape identification.

At the very start I had a feeling—nay, a strong presentiment—that this reckless fellow would disgrace me permanently ere our journey were done; and my impression grew stronger at the tavern in Trenton, where we were forced to stop to warm our numbed limbs, and where I overheard him commanding hot toddy for all the loungers of the bar, and, immediately after, leading the stentorian chorus of a wassail song which made me shudder to the bone.

As if that were not enough, after having wasted half an hour in such a fashion, when we once more set off on our way a score or more of disreputable, red-nosed idlers paraded out in front of the tavern and cheered us, to my supreme embarrassment. Simultaneously, my companion publicly chucked a young maid under the chin.

At that I covered my face completely, and, clapping spurs to my horse's sides, galloped away as fast as could be, for I had acquaintances in Trenton that I would liefer beheld me dead than in such society, or connected with these scandalous goings-on.

The wind had increased to such velocity (shifting its quarter till it blew now in our faces), and we had squandered so much time in the town, that it was after three o'clock of the afternoon when we reached the ferry. Finding ourselves again in motion, on the other side of the Delaware, it came on to snow very hard; and the earth being soon covered with white, the roads became more difficult than before, the drifts rendering the footing treacherous. Nevertheless, we urged forward as fast as able.

I stuck my chin in my collar, and settled upon many improving subjects for the conversations which I would have by Mr. Gray's fireside. I also selected the terms in which to couch my declaration to Miss Sylvia.

These matters determined, I should have turned from my musings, and, despite the unfruitfulness of the soil for good seed, should have essayed an endeavor to inculcate moral principles in the youth beside me; but whenever I opened my mouth to speak the wind flew in so quickly as to take the words back into my throat before they were uttered.

Indeed, the storm had grown fierce to such degree that Fentriss now rode in silence, his face muffled up so that only his eyes showed, though ever and anon he slapped his arms about for warmth, and gave vent to ejaculations the tenor of which I gathered to be anathematical of the weather. Dusk closing in early, our journey became the more difficult, our progress slower and slower. We were nearly overcome with cold, and quite exhausted, when we reached the King George Inn, and, seeking a temporary refuge, thawed our extremities in the tap-room. The landlord warned us against continuing our journey on such a night, but we ventured again into the tempest, deciding to go on to Hoag's Tavern, some five miles distant, where, in case there was no abatement of the external violence, we could spend the night.

It had by this time grown so bitter that no covering afforded protection from the blast, and our horses stumbled wearily as they picked their way through the drifts and over the uneven ground. Darkness fell upon us with a malevolent solidity, like a black bag cast over the head; the wind howled across the fields and shrieked dismally among the trees. The loneliness of the sound, in those terrifying solitudes, would have given rise to a tremor in the stoutest heart, and caused all the idle tales of travellers waylaid and murdered to recur, with appalling force, to the most serious and scholarly mind.

At last, through scudding snowflakes, the welcome lights of Hoag's Tavern shone on our view, and soon after our steeds were munching their fodder in the stable two guest-chambers were being aired and warmed for our slumbers, and we, divested of our boots and outer wrappings, found ourselves seated at a hot supper before a blazing fire.

"So far, and all well," thinks I, congratulating myself as we took our places. "I hope Mr. Gray and Miss Sylvia will not be driven to put in here. That would be a malignant fortune, indeed."

THE STRANGER

"FAITH, Mr. Sudgeberry, it was a wicked wind!" cried Fentriss, hitching his chair closer to the table. "I am sure you have suffered to-day. 'Tis the first time I can recall ever being in your company when you did not beguile each minute with instructive discourse; and it would have brought tears to Mr. Gray's eyes to see you speechless so long. No doubt we shall make up for lost time this evening."

He fell to at the viands with a vivacious appetite, and, I confess, I followed his example; nevertheless, though hungry, I did not confine myself to the satisfaction of purely physical wants, but seized upon the occasion to reprove my *vis-à-vis* for speaking of what was useful and instructive as mere beguilement, and continued by pointing out at length the superior usages that conversation should be put to, far above any mere passing of the time.

We had almost finished our repast, and I was bringing my remarks to a summing-up, when we were interrupted by the arrival of a traveller, who, like ourselves, had been forced to seek shelter from the blast and abandon all hope of continuing his journey till the morrow.

This was a ruddy little man of sixty-five or so, covered with snow from head to foot. He flung his saddle-bags in a corner, shaking off the snow with a great fuss and stamping of his jack-boots; then, in a manner exhibiting considerable flourish, he introduced himself as Mr. O'Donnell, of New York, late of Belfast, travelling to Philadelphia to spend Christmas with a cousin.

He accepted with alacrity William's invitation to join us at table, and, the landlord bringing in fresh supplies, he devoured his victuals with such rapidity and gusto as to overtake us at the last mouthful, by which time I had discovered that he was, as they say, a great talker, one of too voluminous speech; that is, aimlessly prolix, and, a lamentable thing in one of his years, without that sobriety of meaning—inspired by earnestness of purpose alone—which lends grace and dignity to any age. Nay, his talk, though incessant, contained never one rounded period of length and sonorous rendition; his utterances were as jerky as the movements of his active little body.

"And so," he cried, as he wiped the crumbs from his mouth and pushed back his chair—"and so ye tell me ye're a pair of scholars makin' home from the hard study! Aha! Then I've heard of ye!"

"Indeed!" rejoined William. "Mr. Sudgeberry's learning is already famous, then?"

"And so it is!" exclaimed the stranger, leaning back and rubbing his hands hard together, while he looked from one to the other of us and back again, with eyes that twinkled very brightly, like a bird's, in the glow of our heaping fire. In fact, he had just the spryness of a canary, in spite of the bald head and gray fringe of hair that showed his age more plainly when the heat of the room caused him to lay aside the heavy periwig he wore.

"Aha!" he cried. "The gentleman's learning is celebrated to the extent me ears fairly ring with what I'm hearin' of it. But, sirs, I've heard of both of ye."

"Of both of us?" I echoed, mystified.

"Yes, but I have, though—from old man Gray."

"What!" said William, laying down his fork.

"Ha, ha! I thought that was the way of it!" returned the new-comer. "I left New

York this very morning in company with him and his daughter. Aha! which of ye is blushing? Both, be all that's scandalous! Both!"

William had risen to his feet. "Where are they? Where did you leave them? Are they on the road?" he cried. "Do you mean to tell me they risked the—"

Mr. O'Donnell cut him off with a roar of laughter.

"No, no!" he shouted. "Give me a chance till I present the news of it. No, sir. 'Twas yerselves that stopped him—the pair of ye, I mean." He rocked himself in his chair in the throes of enjoyment so exquisite it was nearer agony, and for several moments was unable to continue.

"Which of ye," he sputtered at last—"now, which of ye is the old man hidin' that jew'l of a girl from?"

"What, sir!" cries William. "What, what, what!"

"'Tis just as I'm tellin' ye," answered Mr. O'Donnell. "Old Gray was for pushin' home, spite of storm and wind and all the snow in the world, he was, till we reached the King George Inn, which we did some half-hour after ye'd left it. There the landlord told us two boys from the college, makin' down this way, had gone on to Hoag's for the night. When old Gray heard that, he asked in a hurry was one of them a handsome, gay-lookin' rip with a wicked gray eye, and the other—and the other—"

Here Mr. O'Donnell turned to me with a polite wave of the hand, and again repeating "and the other," was seized with a fit of choking. He scrambled to his feet and walked about the room in evident distress, gasping out, "Pound me on the back!" and, "Let me have it hard!" with various like objurgations between paroxysms, the which instructions William, who had gone to his assistance, carried out heartily. When Mr. O'Donnell grew easier and was somewhat master of himself, he dropped into a chair, whispering weakly, with a wag of his head at me:

"And the other—like yerself, sir!"

"What happened next, if you please?" asked William, anxiously.

"The landlord told him yes, ye were, and Gray swore never another step from the place would he budge the night. That left me to come on alone."

"Then they are at the King George?"

"Where else? Yes, sir—five miles back. The old gentleman said he didn't mind dyin' by storm or freezation. 'It's a comparatively sudden death,' says he, 'and I understand it's painless and easy over. But I'll not risk worse,' says he. 'I've borne all I will of it,' says he, makin' use of some expressions I'll not shock ye with, 'so here we stay the night!' Gentlemen, there was something about his manner—to be frank with ye—that almost led me to conclude that ye're not exactly his favorite scholars; and I believe I should be performin' a sacred duty to warn ye against continuin' whatever it is ye've been doin' to him, because he may work ye harm. He was the desperate-lookin' old man when he said that same!"

William began to pace the floor with hurried steps, but I was plunged into solemn cogitations. Judge of the mixture of my feelings, my sentiments, when I learned that the charming object of my affections was so close at hand, and, indeed, that I should have seen her this very evening at Hoag's except for William Fentriss's presence there; and oh, alas! my mortification that she and her father should learn I was his travelling-companion! Gossip is not always utterly evil, since it was gossip took down William's spirit; but 'tis a very petard, dangerous to the innocent, in the mouth of such a one as that prating old landlord of the King George, a needless babbler whom I loathed with an acute loathing.

"What time does Mr. Gray intend to go on with his journey?" Fentriss inquired, over-carelessly, of Mr. O'Donnell.

"He's up at five in the morning, the mad old ripster, hopin' to get by while ye're still asleep, and looks to be home for to-morrow's breakfast. They start before dawn."

"How does he travel?" asked William.

"How does he travel?" echoed the other. "Faith, then, on the road!"

"No, no; I mean his travelling-carriage. Has he—"

"His own chaise and four."

"Oh!" said William. "Thank you." He paused in his walking the floor, and stood by the chimney-piece regarding the rosy flames attentively, prodding a log-end with his slipper. "Postilion?" he asked.

"Two boys; fine cattle under 'em, sir."

"Ah! Man atop with a blunderbuss?"

"No. The times are not so bad as that, are they?"

"Well," returned Fentriss, reflectively, "there's no telling. The boys have pistols, have they?"

"Have they pistols? Is there an escort of dragoons? Do they carry artillery? And have I fallen in with a couple of highwaymen? Holy powers!" cried our new acquaintance, rising excitedly. "Holy powers! I understand ye! It's an elopement ye're planning!"

"Nay, nay!" exclaimed William, turning a furious crimson, and lifting both hands in protest. "My dear sir—my dear sir—"

"Dear sir, dear sir!" shouted the little man, mocking him. "Don't ye 'dear sir' me! I thought ye were precious solicitous for the old gentleman's safety. Aha! 'A gay-lookin' rip,' says Gray—'a gay-lookin' rip, with a wicked gray eye!' A wicked gray eye! Faith, he knew ye! Aha!"

"Nay, nay!" cried William.

"Ay, ay!" exclaimed the other, dancing across the floor with his hand outstretched to William. "Ay, ay! And upon me immortal soul, what's more, I'm in with ye! I must be counted in! I wouldn't have missed it for all the world and universe. Ye'll find me a great hand at the business, sir. I'm along in years, they'll tell ye, but into every wickedness came near me since the age of five; goin' miles and miles out of me way to embroil meself in any and all dev—"

"This is wild talk!" interrupted William, waving him away.

"So it is!" shouted Mr. O'Donnell. "And what's too wild for a boy like yerself to be plannin'?"

"My dear sir," remonstrated William, "you forget my companion. I believe that you yourself made some allusion to the circumstance that I have the honor to be his rival. Now, I ask you, is it likely that we—"

"What o' that? Can't the two of ye fight it out? Can't ye toss up for yer jew'l, once ye've got her away? Have ye no spurit? Have ye no—"

"Will you hear me?" William broke in, impatiently. "You wrong Mr. Sudgeberry as completely as you misunderstand me. I haven't a ghost of the intention you impute, especially since an elopement would be far from the point, and, if I should—if I should, I repeat—if I should entertain any preposterous and impossible design whatsoever, then, sir, let me tell you that the mere presence of this sober-minded and well-behaved comrade of mine, Mr. Sudgeberry, here, would cause me to abandon it in its conception and be ashamed I *could* conceive it, such is his restraining—nay, his solemn—influence."

Mr. O'Donnell gave a sounding slap to his thigh, went close to William and looked him earnestly in the eye for several seconds, ending with the flicker of one of his eyelids. William's glance wandered to me, then fell, abashed; and at this the other began first to smile and next to laugh.

"Me boy," he cried—"me boy, I like ye," and clapped him on the back with a thump that nigh carried the recipient off his feet. "I like ye! I make no doubt we shall spend as pleasant an evening as the heart could desire, even if ye're not for whippin' away from old Gray with that lovely girl across yer saddle. Let be the elegant storm a-ragin' out-doors, 'tis all the tidier night we'll make within!"

They shook hands, laughing together increasingly, presenting a picture of unseemly merriment, of which I could make nothing, but sat staring at them in wonderment.

"I'm thinkin' I understand ye, Mr. Fentriss," said O'Donnell. "I should offer me very warmest apologies. Such a thing would never enter yer mind. Of course not. Of course it wouldn't. Of course!"

THE CAROUSE

ALL conjectures in regard to the strange hilarity of William and our new acquaintance were cut short by the arrival of the landlord, Hoag, a man of monstrous fatness, who waddled in, bearing a bowl of like corpulence steaming with brown punch, followed by several servants bringing fresh logs for the fire and pipes and tobacco.

"By your leave, gentlemen!" cried the host. "By your leave! You are the only guests in the house to-night, and on such an occasion I hope you'll not think I presume in begging you to be guests *of* the house as well. 'Tis the custom of Hoag's place, and I pray you'll join me in this cheer of Christmas Eve."

If the choice had been left to me, I should have declined the invitation; but my two companions greeted it with unmistakable favor. Mr. O'Donnell, without any words on the matter, sped toward the bowl as if he had been shot at it, filling a cup for himself before it reached the table, and launched a song upon the instant.

"Then *sing!*" He began, loudly:

"Good cheer to him who loves a maid!
Hooroo for him who's not afraid,
For her dear sake,
The laws to break!
We'll sing to him, and yet we say:
Lord save the King and the King's highway!"

"And I give ye the health of me new comrade-in-arms, Mr. Fentriss!" he finished.

Soon, to my vast annoyance, the room was

reeking with the noxious fumes of tobacco, while the rafters rang to the laughter of William, Mr. O'Donnell, and the fat landlord, as they pledged each other (and everything else under the sun) in the hot punch. Mr. O'Donnell was the noisiest little man I ever saw; he trolled forth a dozen catches and ballads of Christmas Eve, one after another, without pause, and followed them up with wanton music—on a comb and paper—of his own composing, he claimed; and well I believed him, for more villanous sounds I never heard.

Finally he turned to me.

"Come, me young Erasmus!" bawls he, as though I had been a mile away. "Join the festivities! Oh, why should the harp on our green hills be silent, and why has me true love no welcome for me? Give us a toast, me joyful—or, can ye sing?"

"Heaven forbid," quoth I, rising, "that I should become a practitioner of levities! Why a series of noises at varying pitches should be held pleasing to the ear has always passed my comprehension. We are now rapidly approaching an age when such barbarous proclivities of the more advanced Caucasian races shall be relegated to those savages from whom they have sprung—an age which every rational intellect must anticipate with symptoms of earnest pleasure."

Thereupon, the landlord, Mr. O'Donnell, and William Fentriss having seated themselves, I branched into a description of the glories of the coming era. I dilated upon the achievements of scholarship, going at length into the researches of science and learning during the last five centuries, and after comparing our present theories with those of the ancients, deduced the results which must inevitably follow (in the future) the trend of modern thought, finally concluding with a carefully correct quotation from a work of infinite merit which exactly coincided with my own views.

Let it never be denied that true learning commands respect even among the most ribald minds: for I was listened to with the most flattering attention. Fentriss, gazing into the fire, appeared to be revolving my observations with profound consideration; Hoag had ensconced himself in the shadow of the chimney-piece, so that he could be discerned only dimly, but his absolute silence betokened entire attentiveness; while little Mr. O'Donnell, favoring me with an extremely polite interest, sat on the edge of his chair and followed my every gesture with open mouth.

As I concluded, he sprang to his feet, and, seizing a candle from the shelf, exclaimed that he must see me to my room himself.

"For," cries he, "I see that ye're worn out and need rest, and our worthy landlord is so immersed in meditation, brought on be the masterly conversation with which we've been favored, that I'll just save him the trouble. Aha! 'Tis the wonderful man ye are, Mr. Sudgeberry! I perform a bit in the same way, meself, but ye're miles and miles ahead of me. Ye've talked for an hour and a half beyond any one I ever heard before! I gathered something of yer powers from what

Mr. Gray said at the King George, but he didn't do ye half justice. He's too old to put it the way it should be, and, besides, his vocabulary is too small for it. It would take a young man—yes, sir, and an athlete at that—in the full possession of his faculties, to describe ye properly, sir. Indeed, sir," he went on to say, as he lighted me up the stairs, "ye've surpassed me wildest expectations of ye, and they were great!"

Then, when he turned to leave me, at the door of my room, he asked, "Me boy, how old are ye?"

"Nineteen," I returned.

"Nineteen!" quoth he. "Nineteen! 'Tis just stupendous! Nineteen! Ah, I'm wishin' I could see ye in yer prime!"

Not without a higher opinion of Mr. O'Donnell, and a fear that I had done him scant justice in my first rating of him, I entered my chamber and prepared for the night.

As I composed my limbs for slumber, my thoughts were divided between regret that my friends had heard of my present association with Fentriss and musings on the delightful meeting of the morrow. Reflecting, however, that my mind might be better employed, I mentally repeated an oration of Cicero, in order to assure myself that, even after the fatigue of the day, my memory retained its customary vigor and accuracy. It is in great part to this diligent habit of my youth that I owe whatever reputation I enjoy to-day. (It would be idle for me to deny that some little talk of me is current beyond our neighborhood.) For of all my parts and faculties, my memory has achieved the most celebration.

Thus occupied, I presently found myself in a fair way to peaceful sleep, when a great disturbance — shouting and laughter, roaring songs, and the clinking of glasses — broke out in the room below, warning me that those pernicious revels, which I congratulated myself I had subdued by a rational conversation, were again in progress.

The tavern was of a shambling construction, walls and floors undeadened, whereby, the room in which the roisterers sat being directly beneath me, I could not fail to catch every sound. And it was not long before my elevated opinion of Mr. O'Donnell had sunk again to an extreme low ebb, and I fell into a great pity for his cousin in Philadelphia and the people at the house he said he was on his way to visit.

Nay, my meditations took a more sombre turn. What assurance had I that the little man was what he represented himself to be? Was there not, indeed, at least a possibility his business might be of so dark a nature that I shuddered to put a name to it? Why had he accompanied the Grays from New York? Why had he not remained at the King George with them? Why had he pushed on down the road ahead of them? Was it, as he had represented, simply to be nearer his destination that he had braved the perils of the storm?

These vague questionings and suspicions (surely not quite unjustified in relation to one who rode alone at night in such weather) were far from being soothed by the nature of the song the little man shouted amid great applause from Fentriss and Hoag, who joined in the chorus.

"I'll now give ye," I heard O'Donnell say—"I'll now give ye a favorite song of the road, and the name of it's called 'The Old Bold Boy.'"

Forthwith he began:

"When the moon swings green
On the hills, I ween,
There's a rider that's shy from view:
He rides in the shade
At the edge o' the glade,
When the lumberin' coach is due.
Bold Boy loves a cloud
On the night, like a shroud,
When the blunderin' coach is due!"

"Chorus: (*Now all of ye join in!*)

"Lord save the King and the King's highway!
Bold Boy he's out till the break o' day.
Good-luck to him and his Fancy, too!
From yokel to bishop
The passengers dish up
The jewels he hangs on his Nancy true.

Me song celebrates him;
The judge elevates him;
Good-luck to him with the grand Hooroo!

"For the dark it's joy
To the Old Bold Boy,
As a-gallopin' out he rides;
And a song he trolls—
(Lord save our souls!
Better larrup the leaders' sides!)
When ye hear that song,
As ye lope along,
Lay the lash to the leaders' sides!"

"Chorus: (*Can't ye make it just a bit louder?*)

"Good cheer to him who loves a maid," and so on.

"How his mare caracoles
At thought of the tolls
He gathers so debonair!
And the mist hangs gray
On the dancing bay,
Like the beards of old men hung there.
On them both hangs the mist,
From fetlock to fist,
Like the beards of old men hung there!"

"Chorus: (*Faith, ye did! Here ye come again.*)

"Lord save the King," and the rest of the rakehelly nonsense.

The chorus was variable, alternating that just quoted with the one sung by Mr. O'Donnell upon the entrance of the punch-bowl. He bellowed eleven or twelve stanzas of this ominous ditty, and the others joined the chorus each time, with a palpable intention to raise the roof, the punch having gone to their lungs.

Song succeeded song, ballad followed ballad, chorus begat chorus. It was marvellous how three men could make so much noise and so persistently. They kept it up till I thought the pangs of exhaustion must have caused them to cease, but the passage of hours only appeared to increase their vigor. Meanwhile, the depth of my indignation (supplanting all alarms) may be imagined. For a long time I tossed from side to side, until, quite worn out with the effort to obtain relief in slumber, I lay on my couch in distress too great to move another inch.

The only respite I obtained was for half an hour or so, during which the three held an earnest conversation in very low tones. The tenor of it I could not determine, though ever and anon they gave vent to delirious chucklings and exclamations. Once I heard the landlord mention my own name, and Fentriss assuring him that I was long since sound asleep, and tired enough to snore until late in the morning. Hoag left the party after this, and I heard him hallooing in the hall, as if to awaken sleepers:

"Bates! Bates! Hi, Nick and Tom and the rest of you! You're wanted. Hi, Bates!"

Soon I made out that he returned with four or five men who walked with heavy steps, servants about the inn, I supposed, hostlers or what not. They were invited to fill their glasses, complying with great laughter and a hoarse song to Christmas, following which Mr. O'Donnell sang his song of the road again—twice!

The addition of the low party to the company, and their all joining in toasts and singing, produced a hubbub which was like utterly to confound my feverish brain. At last exhausted nature claimed her own, and, in spite of the goings-on beneath me, I dropped into a painful stupor, not to be called sleep, but a state nearer a swooning perturbation of the whole being than slumber, and troubled by malignant visions. More as it were in dreams than in reality, it seemed a semi-quiet fell in the room below; after that a sound of feet stumbling over the whole house, in every part and division of it, and of doors flung open and slammed to. One called loudly for his boots, and Fentriss's voice said, "Hush!" Another fell over a chair and cried out with vehemence.

Then all was still, and I had a long dream of a battle wherein I suffered greatly.

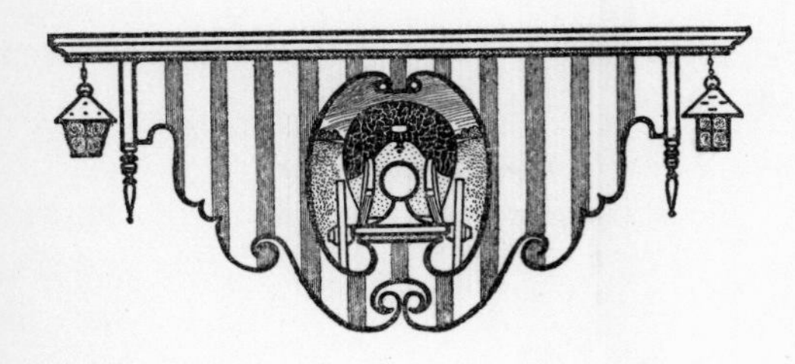

MR. SUDGEBERRY'S RECKLESS HUMOR

METHOUGHT I was unable to stir from the point of contact between two great regiments of horse, charging down on each other, while they thundered this chorus:

> "For her dear sake,
> The laws to break!
> We'll sing to him, and yet we say:
> Lord save the King and the King's highway!"

but at the crucial moment I saved myself by

waking with a jump so sudden that it seemed to stop my heart. Fear was still upon me; I found my back a-creep with cold and all my being alert to unknown horrors closing in on me through the darkness.

Everything was silent—silent! I sat up in bed and listened.

> "Bold Boy he's out till the break o' day."

There came faintly to my hearkening ear the murmur, like a failing echo, of that satanic chorus, as if it came from far down the road:

> "Good-luck to him with the grand Hooroo!"

The suspicions I had entertained of O'Donnell sprang up full-armed in my mind, bearing with them thoughts so wild that a fit of sinking, deep in my inwards, was their accompaniment. When I had mastered my emotions somewhat, I had a vivid, painful apprehension that there was a strange presence in the room, the which conception finally growing so intolerable that I crept out of the covers strategically, went to the door, and felt to see if it could be still bolted. All was secure.

Returning cautiously toward the bed, I overturned a chair. It fell like a church.

The noise of it in the hush ran through the house in a ghastly resonance, seeming to rattle the doors of a hundred empty rooms for admission. I stood stock-still, and the renewed silence was as startling as the noise had been.

Then again, as I stood there, I heard the murmur of the highwayman's chorus, farther away, fainter:

> "Me song celebrates him;
> The judge elevates him!"

I tiptoed to the window and looked out. The tempest had long since passed; the night was clear and brilliant with stars over great wastes of snow. In the distance I made out a dark patch against the vasty white, a blur of shifting shape.

This blur was moving slowly, steadily northward. I peered long into the distance;

my sight grew clearer, and I saw what it was: a group of men and horses. They were going up the road — the significant and sinister thought flashed into my mind—*toward the King George Inn!*

Not daring to risk a candle, I began to grope for my garments, and to get them upon me as rapidly as was consistent with complete noiselessness, shivering with unspeakable misgiving at the least rustling caused by my haste and the darkness. It was impossible to find all my apparel under such conditions; indeed, I put forth no efforts toward a toilet, being occupied more acutely with considerations of an apprehensive character.

What *was* Hoag's Tavern? Could it be one of those ominous hostelries where men entered but departed never?

I had not stopped at the place before, nor, on my passing by, had I done better than merely to note its existence. I remembered no word of its repute. Who and what was the landlord? What connection had he with O'Donnell? And into what plot had they persuaded the weak, the reckless Fentriss?

Was it possible that they had decoyed him to his destruction? or had *he*, giving way to the desperation of a despised suitor, and welcoming any mad deed as a relief from his own thoughts, bribed and persuaded them to some contemplated violence?

Above all these grewsome interrogations there rose one of anguished self-reproach: Why had I — O ill-considering youth!— rushed so blindly into the unknown, entering this strange inn, which might be a law-breakers' rendezvous for aught I knew, without question or cavil, incautiously walking to my not impossible doom, alone and defenceless?

They had gone up the road toward the King George Inn—what had they left in the house for me?

As this disquieting suggestion assailed me, I looked down from the window; it was too long a drop for safety; the mere thought of attempting such a thing was loathsome to my soul; and I had no more confidence in a rope of bedclothes than in my ability to construct one, or to descend it, supposing it made. Hence I must make my way out through the house; for I had settled in my mind to get out-of-doors by some means—waiting there in the darkness for what might happen was too horrid to consider. Therefore, summoning the greatest degree of fortitude consistent with the occasion, I stealthily slid the bolt, and, opening the door, stole out upon the landing in my stockinged feet.

Here I remained a considerable time, motionless, though the landing was very cold. Without warning, a hideous creak came from the stairs below, and I leaped back into my room, closed and bolted the door again. Then, after some minutes, concluding that the sound had been caused by the chill in the wood, I issued anew. Twice more did the creaking oblige me to seek refuge within, but at last very desperation called upon my will and I descended the stairs, stepping twice on each one, shivering from head to heel, the back of my neck seeming to twitch with apprehensions of danger in the rear.

At the foot of the stairway a patch of faint light browned the black floor, falling through the open door of the chamber where the revels had been indulged. Now, employing infinite stealth, I pressed my body close against the wall in the shadow, and crooking my neck so that only the top of my head and my eyebrows might be visible to any occupant if he chanced to gaze at the spot where they appeared (which I had hopes he might not do), I spied within.

No one was there. Only blank disorder met my gaze: the empty punch-bowl broken on the floor; the fire a heap of smouldering ashes; the cloth stained and awry; chairs were upset; the one remaining candle burned low in its socket; everywhere was the dreariest confusion, but all a-brooding with a quiet which awed my soul. Nevertheless, something in that fateful hush—I know not what—gave me assurance that the whole house was as empty as the room before my eyes. From the bar the ticking of the tall timepiece could be heard — the only sound except my breathing. The hour sounded. It was five o'clock, and Christmas morning.

Taking the candle, I peered into the rooms on each hand, into the hall and kitchen; not a mouse was stirring. Finding my boots in the kitchen, I drew them on, lit a lantern, and crept out of that deserted tavern by the back way, following the path to the stables.

All about me the snow was trampled as by a regiment, and what was my horror to find the stables as barren of life as the house! Nay, for here not only man was missing, even the beasts were absent; not a horse was in the place; my own Jeremiah, my last hope of safety, gone with the rest!

Upon this discovery an uncomfortable perspiration burst out of all my pores; the sinking spell in my inwards immediately followed, so that I was forced to sit upon a heap of straw to collect my faculties.

Now, in ruminating upon the painfulness

of my situation, as I spied about the house, I had reached a certain conclusion; also I had formed a determined resolution, the latter being hopelessly foiled by the absence of Jeremiah and all other horses. This was the conclusion, and I had no doubt of its correctness: an attack upon Mr. Gray's carriage had been meditated, agreed to, and was now in process of execution, with the abduction and kidnapping of Miss Gray by William Fentriss as part of a design which might include the murder of her good old father.

My resolution was: to saddle my horse, then, taking the opposite direction from the scene of conflict, to speed down the road until I reached the first house whence I could send back aid to the imperilled chaise, while I hastened on to inform the authorities.

Now, here was I left by those horse-robbing villains not only without the means for such a course, but at the mercy of the first wretch to return. My blood paused in its circulation as I thought of the aged but reckless O'Donnell or the powerful Hoag.

A daring idea entered my head as I sat there in the straw. 'Twas a conception so foolhardy as to cause my flesh to creep, one which my soberer judgment condemns as the rash project of a youth of nineteen. This was to reconnoitre—going *toward* the impending violence, mind you, instead of away from it! Yet, favored by fortune, I believed I might hope to come through with my life, the more as it was quite dark and I was under no necessity to approach the rascals within pistol-shot. Also, a four-foot hedge ran along the east side of the road, and it was my intention to creep forward in its shelter, though the hedge was a thorny one, to hearing distance of the conflict, if possible.

Such was the wildness of the mood which now took possession of me.

THE DOGS OF WAR

I BLEW out my lantern, stole forth to the road, and began to grope through the snow behind the hedge. My heart thumped with excitement, while ever and anon, the perilous case in which I stood coming with great vividness to my mental vision, I paused and reviewed the risk I ran.

But my reckless humor returned each time, and with the low-muttered words, "It is all for Sylvia!" on I pressed.

My progress was slow, the snow having piled high on the hither side of the hedge, and so unevenly that several times I stumbled and measured my length in its depths, when it filled the tops of my boots and penetrated every aperture in my hastily donned apparel. A great quantity appeared to have wormed its way inside my collar, where it lay without my having the power to dislodge it, and, melting, ran down my back; added to this, my head was very cold, my nightcap affording insufficient protection, for I had been unable to discover my hat.

In such discomfort, my teeth chattering the while, I had accomplished some three-quarters of a mile or so, when I unfortunately fell into a wide ditch which ran through the field.

I was proceeding somewhat cautiously on hands and knees at the time, and it was in that posture that I found myself plunging through a brittle lid of thin ice and floundering in the water. More dead than alive, I got to my feet and spluttered my way out on the other side, with the words, "For Sylvia's and old Mr. Gray's sakes!" on my lips.

As I climbed up the farther bank there was a sudden loud shout from the road, not ten feet away. Startled as I was, I recognized the voice as that of William Fentriss. There was an answering cry from above, and a man forced his horse close to the hedge and peered into the darkness.

Apprehending, not without reason, a third spell of that dreadful sinking, I crept close under the bushes and lay still, while the streams of water running from every portion of my attire melted the snow in all directions.

"Will, me boy," called the second voice, which I was at no loss to attribute to the terrible O'Donnell, "have ye fell in the brook?"

"No," returned the other. "Some animal must have blundered in."

"Some animal!" cried O'Donnell. "Do ye have hippopotami wandering over the fields in this country?"

"I haven't heard of it, noble captain."

"I'm thinkin' 'twas a pair of them," went on O'Donnell—"or more like a drove, be the splashin' of 'em. Keep yer eye open for a few elephants, then! Where's me mask? I'm off to take command of me merry men. Ha, ha! Cap'n Blacknight and his bloodthirsty crew!"

He set his horse in motion and cantered up the road, while my veins stagnated at his sinister words.

"Be careful of your gallant roan, captain," William called after him.

"Aha! the steed of young Erasmus!" the villain yelled in return.

It was too true: the Irish criminal had stolen my horse, lending his own to some other member of the band. I trembled for poor Jeremiah in such unhallowed hands, but all the resources of my intelligence were immediately required by the danger of my own situation; for Fentriss, leaning over the hedge, looking for the supposed animal, presently discharged a pistol at a small bush near me.

My first impulse was to cry out and warn him that I was no lurking beast, but the words froze tight ere they left my throat, as the thought struck me with terrific force that William's desperation must be a thousandfold increased by the knowledge that he had a human—instead of a brute—witness of his enterprise, and I saw no hope in appealing to his friendship. Nay, I feared that any declaration of my presence might render his aim only more accurate.

My position was clearly untenable; every movement engendered a crisis. With Fentriss and the ditch cutting off all escape to the rear, and the cut-throat band threatening my front, which way was I to turn? The pistol-shot decided the question for me.

I began at once to creep forward, and, as soon as I deemed it comparatively safe, to run, still leaning close to the hedge—so close, indeed, as to leave particles of my wearing apparel upon its thorny projections, several times being separated from areas of such extent they might have been considered almost indispensable; my face and hands also suffered extraordinarily from scratches. Meanwhile, my brain was in a tumult of confusion, a thousand questions surging through it. Was the abduction of Miss Gray the only design of the scoundrels? Why was Fentriss left behind? Did their plan include robbery or murder, or both? Why had I been so venturesome? Why, oh, why?

Why had I not remained in the stable and waited under a pile of straw for daylight? There was plenty of straw there. But here, where my recklessness had driven me, was only a prickly hedge, and the growing light would not save but ruin me with its hideous revelation of my position — caught between two fires! In the east there was already a sombre glow; the western skies, responding with long, red streaks, betokened the approach of dawn, while the horizonal stars waxed paler every moment.

Suddenly I heard a shrill whistle blown from the road, near by. At the sound I dropped (almost involuntarily) flat on my face, then, peering through a minute gap in the hedge, what was my horror to find I had run full into the nest of them.

I recognized O'Donnell by my unhappy Jeremiah, and the treacherous landlord, Hoag, on account of his monstrous girth, though all faces were masked with black cloth. Their followers were distributed on both sides of the road, every man leaning forward in his saddle, listening intently.

"Hark!" said the landlord.

From the distance came the faint cry of a postilion urging his leaders; and then, carried on the wintry air, a few bars of a lively Christmas song blown on the post-horn.

"Aha!" shouted O'Donnell, exultantly. "Take yer places, me knights of the road!"

"Don't put me too much in the thick of it, cap'n," whispered Hoag, plucking at the other's arm. "I'm a well-known man and easy recognized."

"Stay back a bit, then," replied O'Donnell. "But ye must bear a good hand in the noise."

"Trust me for that," answered Hoag,

wheeling his horse about. "I'll do more than any ten men alive!"

He rode over and reined in so close to the spot where I lay that I scarce dared breathe, for I could hear plainly his own asthmatic wheezing. My uneasiness was thus augmented at every turn; the man was actually almost over my head; indeed, I could have touched his stirrup by passing my hand through the hedge without moving the rest of my body. He had an old, bell-mouthed blunderbuss across his saddle, and flourished a long cutlass, wearing no sheath that I could discover.

O'Donnell, with two others, rode slowly forward about thirty paces; three more followed them at a slight distance.

Then I realized that the chaise had drawn much nearer; and, though it was still unseen, we could hear it coming on at a clipping gait. As the sounds which heralded its approach fell clearer on the ear, mine heart seemed like to burst, so great was the flopping of it.

We could hear the postilion carolling, and urging his horses between snatches of song.

We could hear the creak of the heavy wheels over the snow, the rattle of harness, the clinking of chains; we heard the rapid, muffled hoof-beats of the four; and now, with tossing heads, and the snow flying from their heels, they swept round a turn in the road and were upon us.

There rang out on the frosty air a shout: "Stand and deliver!"

To my horror, the villain O'Donnell fairly hurtled my poor Jeremiah and himself against the leaders; and his immediate followers pursued the same tactics, instantaneously launching their assault. The chaise stopped with a shock; the leaders reared; one boy was flung off; the plunging four were swung into the hedge, while the brigands of the reserve wheeled into line across the road.

The second postilion, knocked from his horse in mid-act to draw a pistol, was immediately bound to a tree; but there came a shot from the interior of the vehicle; a woman's scream was also heard in that quarter, together with an expression of outraged astonishment and indignation couched in a vocabulary which caused me to shudder for old Mr. Gray's future.

What followed was such a confusion and passed so quickly as to beggar all description. Suffice it to say that the ruffians who had assailed the chaise forthwith let out such a bawling and raised such an uproar and din as no mortal ever heard before. They discharged their pistols in the air, and hammered the sides of the carriage with hangers and cutlasses, keeping up a most horrid clamor and tumult the while.

In all my agony of mind I found time to puzzle at such lunatic conduct on the part of highwaymen. It passed my comprehension.

By far the most successful at this ear-splitting was that scoundrel landlord Hoag, so near whom it was my misfortune to have made my hiding-place. He began to discharge his piece as fast as he could load, letting it off in every direction under the sun, now in the air overhead, now in the hedge within a yard of my body, so that (having no cognizance that it was not charged with ball) I gave up all for lost; and at the same time he set up a heathenish bellowing and howling and hideous screaming and squealing, the like never heard outside a mad-house.

The others, completely beside themselves with envy of his prowess, put forth their utmost powers to outdo him, and then, indeed, such pandemonium reigned there on the road, that cold Christmas morning, as would have convinced a passer-by he witnessed an orgy of Hades.

Suddenly, from down the way, we heard a great cry:

"A rescue! A rescue!"

A single horseman came galloping up the road, the snow flying out in a cloud behind him and the reins flung over his horse's neck. He flourished a long rapier in one hand, a pistol in the other, his hat was blown off, and his cloak flapped like a black wing with the speed of his coming.

"Hold, curs!" he thundered. *"Turn, dogs, and meet your doom!"*

Then, discharging his pistol, he flew into the dark mass of combatants about the chaise.

It was William Fentriss!

THE DOUBLE VILLAIN

WITH the advent of William the uproar redoubled.

A more furious clashing of steel and sound of buffeting, combined with grewsome shrieking and heart-rending groans, was not heard at Blenheim when the French and English horse met by the tens of thousands. Up and down the road, across and over, all round the chaise, the combat raged, with the horrible and prodigious noises ever increasing, while inside the vehicle old Mr. Gray never once ceased from his frightful profanity throughout the engagement.

A thousand cries pierced the ear:

"Ha! have at you, then!" "Back, Sir Lionel, back!" and the like. *"So, caitiff!" "No quarter!" "Dog, we shall meet again!"*

But over all the fearsome hullabaloo, rose a voice I knew for O'Donnell's in spite of his attempt to disguise it:

"Fly! fly, me boys! This fiend is invincible! Away, or we are all dead men! Back to the cave to count our losses!"

"Fly! fly!" cried the others, and, *"Don't forget the wounded!"* and, *"Back to the cave!" "Escape! escape!"*

They wheeled about with a great clatter and screams of fear. The rascally Hoag let off his blunderbuss for a last time, almost directly over my head, so that my nightcap was burned full of holes from sparks and my face so diabolically blackened with the discharge that my nearest relatives might not have known me, and whole days elapsed before I rid myself of the traces. In addition to this outrage, the scoundrel had so infuriated his horse by the inhuman disturbance he raised that when he endeavored to turn and join his fellow-conspirators in their flight, the maddened beast reared up on his posterior limbs, then plunged, and the huge bulk of the innkeeper crashed down through the hedge and landed with extraordinary force at my feet. At the same time, with the sound of a smothered laugh and of galloping hoof-beats through the snow, the other ruffians made off down the road and were gone.

William was setting the postilions at liberty (for both boys had been trussed up) when I heard a sound most unlike those which had so horridly assailed us. It was the light and mellow voice of Sylvia, and it shook, not with fear, but with the vibrant thrill of sweeter agitations.

She had sprung from the chaise and was standing by the steps, both hands outstretched toward Fentriss.

"Will!" she cried. "Will!"

He turned to her, and started.

"*You!*" he said. "Ah, how I have waited!"

This brought me to my feet instantly.

"Oh, double villain!" I shouted. "Oh, unconscionable reprobate!"

They did not hear me, nor in that gray light take note of me.

I pressed hard into the hedge to break through, regardless of being stuck by the thorns, beginning to shout again, but I had not half the word "unconscionable" out of my mouth when I was clasped about the middle and flung to earth beneath the weight of the landlord, I on my face, the ponderous miscreant on my back.

"Hush!" he whispered, angrily. "All's safe if we lay by, now. What on earth were you doing?"

"*Help!*" I shouted, but he clapped his hand over my mouth and held me down, though I strove frantically to rise.

"Hold your tongue!" he whispered. "What

do you mean? It's me, it's Hoag; there's nothing to fear. Would you spoil the fun now, when we've carried all out so nobly, and the young man so liberal to you lads? Why didn't you ride ahead? Were you thrown, too? It's Bates, isn't it?"

He took his hand from my mouth, and I attempted to raise another shout, but he buried my face in the snow so suddenly by a shove of his hand on the top of my head that only a brief gurgle was allowed to issue from me.

"Ha!" exclaimed the landlord. "'Tis the punch, is it? Then I'll hold you fast till they're gone, as a warning not to take such advantage of a free bowl next time!" And he plunged me deeper into the snow.

Next, that all should be secure, he skewed about, raised himself up quickly, and, before I had time to squirm from under, came down upon me, sitting, mostly upon my head—an attitude as comfortable for himself as it was painful and disrespectful to me.

Only my anger prevented me from swooning through the miseries of my situation, knowing that my perfidious rival was receiving the homage due a hero, while I, powerless to prevent, must lie, not ten yards away, choking with the snow and rage, under that monstrosity, Hoag!

"In, in with you, my boy!" I heard Mr. Gray cry, heartily. "You must ride with Sylvia. I never knew such heroism!"

"But my horse," said William.

"*I'll* take your horse," answered the trusting dotard. "Not a word — not a word! Heavens! Heavens! but who ever saw such swordsmanship! Now, lads, halloo, then! On! on!"

The postilions called, "Ay, ay! Very good, sir!" They spoke to the horses, and I underwent the agony of hearing the cavalcade move forward.

"There!" said Hoag. "You'd have made a fine mess of it, wouldn't you! You ought to be whacked for risking a betrayal of the gentleman; and if you're forgiven, it 'll be for the day's sake, and because of the royal Christmas Eve at Hoag's."

A prodigious chuckling shook its way through all the puffy flanges of his person. "Ha, ha! Of all the wild nights I ever spent! But the fun of it! Ha, ha! Oh, law—me! Hark! So, then, they're gone," he continued, as the noise of the chaise grew fainter in the distance. "There! You may get up, Bates."

He slowly removed himself from me, but did not rise; instead, he merely rolled over to the hedge in a burst of laughter.

"Bates!" he cried. "Bates! if you was only sober, and intelligent when sober, the fun of this night would be the death of you, as it's like to be of me! That mad rogue, that young Fentriss! Who but one like him, and that ripping, tearing, rearing old O'Donnell—who but such as them could ha' thought out and performed such a plan! And old Gray! Did you hear him in the chaise? Did you *hear*— Oh, ho, ho, ho! Oh, law—me! Ha, ha, ha, ha!"

I brought his roaring to a sudden end.

The cutlass he had carried during the engagement had spun over the hedge ahead of him when he fell, and no sooner did he release me than I made myself its master. This done, I came and stood over him, my indignation too great for utterance. I looked down at the shaking, shouting mass of flesh with no more fear of it than of a kitten, for now, at last, I understood the heinous plottings of the night. No, it was not fear moved in my bosom, but an overwhelming, a righteous, and an all-devouring wrath. As the first measure of justice, the huge calf of the landlord's leg striking my eye temptingly, without hesitation I lowered the point of the cutlass, and, although his hilarious floppings-about made the feat somewhat difficult to perform, caused its point to penetrate the flesh; whereat he left off laughing with a surprising shriek, and sat up against the hedge abruptly, rubbing his leg and staring at me with a countenance of the utmost ruefulness and consternation.

"Villain!" I cried, and threatened him with my sword again.

"It ain't Bates!" he whispered, huskily. "It ain't Bates!"

"Villain!"

"Who is it?" he asked, appealingly. "Tell me who it is."

"Rascal, you know me well enough," cried I.

"No, no," he answered, with a frightened look. "Is it a nigger?" The light was growing stronger; he could see me plainly, but still gazed upon me from head to foot with a bewildered and wondering air.

"Who is it?" he repeated.

"You thought me abed, but I have been a witness to the whole villany."

"Abed — abed!" he rejoined, vacantly. "But I never saw you before."

I menaced him again with the weapon.

"No more of this! And now, sin-laden and over-zealous sergeant of Diabolus," I thundered, "only one thing can save you from the gallows you have richly merited: that is my intervention, contingent upon your public confession, as I direct; nor, if you refuse, shall you know mercy or mitigation!"

His eyes protruded from their sockets and his hands went up over his head as high as his fat arms could lift them.

"Lord deliver us!" he gasped. "'Tis Mr. Sudgeberry!"

THERE CAME ONE SHRIEKING "JUSTICE!"

THE day was coming on broad and clear as the landlord and I went down the road toward the inn, he walking a pace in front, under compulsion of the cutlass, and limping somewhat, partly from soreness and partly because he grew more and more loath to proceed, while ever and anon he turned a look of pleading over his shoulder.

"But, Mr. Sudgeberry," quoth he, "it was only after—"

Whereupon I would cut him off sharply and threaten him in flank with the cutlass. Thus I drove him on, and I did not forget to improve the time by delivering a severe discourse to him upon the end of the wicked, pointing out the evils of punch-drinking with loose companions, and the pitfalls that besiege the unwary who listen to the counsels of the dissolute.

At first he had been prone to uncontrollable gusts of laughter every time his eye fell upon me, or whenever I sneezed. (The latter affliction frequently convulsed my person, for my souse in the brook had given me a violent cold in the head, the which likewise engendered a difficulty of enunciation, so pronounced that I was forced to render all sounds of *M* and *N* as though they were *B* and *D*—a circumstance I mention out of a fear that some might fail to comprehend the total of what was inflicted upon me that night, but not here to be transcribed lest the potency of my utterances be lost in confusion.) Long before I finished, the landlord had grown sober and plaintive near to the point of tears.

"Oh, that punch!" he exclaimed, shaking his head ruefully. "'Twas it led me into this business. Never again will I touch a drop of punch! Ah, but surely you don't mean—"

"I don't mean!" I cried, hastening him on with a whack from the flat of the cutlass. "I don't mean! You will see! Meanwhile, you are going straightway with me to Mr. Gray and his daughter, or I hale you before the nearest magistrate on a charge of attempted robbery by force and arms on the king's highway!"

He was red by habit; now he became sickly yellow, and remained so. "Law! law! 'Twas but a hodgepodge of a jest. What harm in the world was in it, Mr. Sudgeberry? Now, why disgrace Mr. Fentriss, and belike ruin me and my house, for this little—"

"Confession or the gallows!" I answered, with so inexorable a mien that he looked even sicklier than before; and there was nothing like laughter in the man; he could only groan out useless explanations and protests, saying, over and over, "But we thought you sound asleep, safe abed, sir," as if that completely excused his execrable conduct.

I continued to threaten him with both the weapon in my hand and the terrors of the law until, as we approached the inn, his great body seemed too much weight for his knees, and he was but a heap of flesh and sorrow.

"Confession is your only salvation!" I exclaimed, repeatedly. "Otherwise you climb the gallows steps. Hasten! We follow them to Mr. Gray's, instantly."

"Ah, now if you'd but listen!" he expostulated. "Mr. Fentriss is your friend; this will destroy him if you proceed with it. You can't mean to do him such an ill turn!"

"Not another word. We stop only for horses, and ride straight after them."

"There's no need, if you're set on this cruelty," he answered, hanging his head like the shamed man he was. "They are at the tavern. Mr. Fentriss promised beforehand he would persuade them to stop there for breakfast and recuperation. But surely you won't punish us so hard for a jest which we did not mean should include you or be of hurt to anybody; and for my part I was only talked into it after—"

I bade him be silent, and sternly drove him on, my choler mounting higher and higher, not lessened by imaginings of that arch-hypocrite, William, reinstated with the Grays by this false rescue. I saw him, the deceiver and traitor, receiving the adulation due a hero, and ensconced in shadowy corners with Miss Sylvia during the holidays, while I was left to perform the unmerited task of renewing my conversations for the benefit of the aged father alone. *No!* A thousand times no! William Fentriss was in my power; and how well he deserved to be humbled and exposed for all time!

There sounded a call from ahead, and I was aware of a horseman who made his approach at a rapid gait. Taking off his hat with a flourish, he disclosed to our eyes the features of the ribald O'Donnell. He was mounted on his own horse, his saddle-bags betokening his intention to continue his journey.

He hailed the innkeeper with a shout:

"We missed ye, Hoag, and I placed meself at the head of a reconnoitrin' party, consistin' of meself, to look for ye. Saints and martyrs! What black tatterdemalion have ye there?"

He squinted his eyes and stared at me, astonished.

"Are ye captive to a blackamoor, or are ye just towin' a gentleman got up for a masquerade?"

"Pay no attention to him or you suffer from my steel!" I said, savagely, to Hoag. "Have you not already followed the malevolent advisings of the meddlesome and mischievous to your present undoing? Concentrate your mind upon your miseries, and—"

"Be the gods of perdition, 'tis me little

man!" cried O'Donnell, reining back. "Young Erasmus! No! Yes! No! Upon me soul, it is, it *is!* 'Tis that marvellous bird a-drivin' our quadruplex Bacchus be force and arms at the point of the sword, and as disfigured as St. Peter's toe!"

He rode up beside us. "What in the world has happened to ye, me Achilles? And what has Hector done that ye drag him round the walls in ignominy and disgrace?" He seemed utterly taken aback.

"Go your ways, *Captain Blacknight!*" I answered, grimly. "And be glad that you escape the scaffold. This wretch comes with me to make his confession to the unprotected old man whose carriage you so treacherously assaulted."

"Ha, ha!" shouted the disreputable Irishman. "Is that the tune of it? And so ye weren't abed, after all, me little Achilles! Sure I'd like to be stoppin' to see, for there'll be warm times at the inn, I'm takin' me oath! Give me love to Mr. Gray, and pass him me compliments on his noble powers of swearin', and on the elegant new son-in-law he's gettin' for a Christmas present!"

"What do you mean?" I demanded.

"Sure, one of ye is bound to be selected," he answered, "and I'm thinkin' that same 'll take place this very mornin'. Good-luck to ye both!" he concluded, "and God help the old man!"

Deigning no reply, I ordered Hoag to march on, offering him, if he did not, a thwack from the cutlass, but the Irishman urged his horse across our path.

"Beggin' pardon for me interferin' disposition," he said. "Landlord, me reckonin' is paid. And — man, do ye want a rescue?"

Hoag only shook his head gloomily.

"Then I wish ye a merry Christmas!" cried O'Donnell, wheeling about. "Come to see me when ye visit New York, Mr. Sudgeberry. I've some friends there that I wouldn't have miss ye for the world. Merry Christmas! The merriest Christmas that ever was to ye both!"

With that, laughing in utter shamelessness, he rode away. I looked to see him stop at the inn to warn Fentriss; but we were now close on; he appeared to think better of it, so, with a wave of his hand, he clapped heels to his horse's sides and was gone.

Smoke came pouring out of the chimneys of the tavern; ruddy fires shone through the window-panes; and in the stable-yard Mr. Gray's chaise (with most of the varnish knocked off) stood waiting, while the horses were being led to and fro. As we entered the main door I saw that everything had been made bright, clean, and cheery. A smug barmaid stood ready to courtesy; men-servants bustled in and out, bearing steaming dishes, or ran here and there with fresh logs of firewood; for the knaves had learned their lessons well, and, in spite of the absence of their master, had fled straight from the assault to the inn, where, no doubt, they had greeted the travellers' tale of the attack with the neatest innocence and wonderment.

The landlord exhibited an almost violent

reluctance to go in, but I overcame his objections with another reference to the law and his own crime. In fact, having no more fear of him, from the moment of his first fright, than of a calf, I gave him another poke with my sword, upon which his resistance collapsed utterly, and he passed in-doors in a state of piteous dejection.

At sight of us the bar-maid emitted a scream, and covered her face with her apron; a man carrying a great platter of eggs and bacon dropped it to the floor; two other knaves, variously laden, staggered back in consternation, giving way before us; and without more ado I stepped to the door of the room in which we had supped the preceding evening. It stood one-quarter ajar. The landlord came to a halt, turning his head to me in a last mute appeal to proceed no farther, and I paused to look within.

The scene which met my gaze was cosey, appetizing, warmly lit by the fire on the hearth and by the long, horizontal rays of the sun, which now shone red on the windows. The fresh, white cloth sparkled with its load of cutlery and china. Never was completer comfort seen, nor three cheerier people than those who sat before me.

Mr. Gray was ensconced upon one side of the table, applying himself heartily to a dish of cutlets, while opposite him, neglecting the viands before them, and with chairs whose proximity I instantly marked, sat that false conspirator and Miss Sylvia. The deep blush which suffused her brow, as she hearkened to his cooing, was near the color of the ribbons she wore, for her travelling-cloak was unclasped, and at her throat I caught the flicker of those cherry ribbons which I still so strangely remember—those cherry ribbons which she flaunted both this winter morning and that other day in June.

As for my feelings at sight of the happy party, I choked with indignation and just wrath to see them all so comfortable, especially the villain who had caused the trouble. He looked as fresh and neat as if he had just risen from an honest slumber on a Sabbath morning, while I, for *his* sins, must needs present a mere wreck to the familiar eye.

The pretended paladin was gazing at Miss Sylvia with all his eyes, as if so hungry for the sight of her he meant to make up for months of absence in one morning's looking. Ay, although I saw that attitude for but an instant, it had this in it, and more—something which brought me to the immediate conclusion that I had arrived no better than just in time: a half-tremulous smile was on his lips, the smile of a man who sees coming to him, only a moment or an inch away, the greatest happiness of his life.

My indignation became so unbearable that I could but reach out and prod the wretched Hoag again, which (as it came upon him unexpectedly) caused him to give forth a vehement cry of misery. Then I flung the door wide open, urged the wailing landlord before me by flagellations with the flat of my cutlass, and stood upon the threshold.

I levelled a justly vengeful forefinger at William Fentriss, and, conquering a spell of sneezing, cried, loudly,

"Behold a perfidious monster!"

MR. SUDGEBERRY AND THE CHERRY RIBBONS

THE three occupants of the room turned toward the door and stared at us in a kind of paralytic amazement for several moments, during which my renewed sneezing was the only sound to be heard.

It was Miss Sylvia who first recovered. She rose to her feet with a slight scream; Mr. Gray dropped knife and fork clattering upon his plate; and William sprang up with a sharp exclamation. It was a sweet sop to my rage to see the change come over Mr. Fentriss when his gaze rose to the disclosure of his Nemesis! He gave a wretched look at us, which took in the broken posture of the dilapidated innkeeper, my tattered nightcap, smeary cheeks, wrathful brow, and the cutlass; and in the stern picture he read his fate.

He staggered back against the wall with his hand across his eyes, as if a sudden vertigo had seized him. Then he made one gesture of intense appeal, seemingly begging to be spared the humiliation so properly in store for him; but as he saw the uselessness of it, his arms dropped to his sides, and he stood, with head fallen and shoulders bowed, like one already condemned and lost.

I advanced into the room with a solemn tread.

"What is this?" gasped Mr. Gray. "Another robbery?"

"Behold a perfidious monster!" I repeated, still pointing at William Fentriss across the

"MISS SYLVIA ROSE TO HER FEET WITH A SLIGHT SCREAM"

table. At the sound of my voice, Miss Gray shrieked aloud.

"Heaven defend us!" exclaimed her father. "'Tis that Sudgeberry!"

Miss Gray fell back in her chair and covered her face with her hands.

"Ay, old man," I answered, in a fateful tone, in spite of the before-mentioned infirmity of pronunciation which forced me to address him, against my will, as "old bad," instead of "old man," although I had then no desire to speak harshly to him, "it is I!"

"It *is!*" he cried. "What in the name—"

"I am come to defend you, white-haired and credulous old man," I continued, raising my voice. "I am come to defend you from the embraces of a monster who has played upon your guileless nature and upon that of this innocent maiden, your daughter, even as he played upon his villanous musical instruments last summer. I am here to expose the wiles of a traitor who has caused you to imperil your soul by your profanity, and who, by unheard-of trickery, has sought to reopen the sacred portals of your household, entrance to whose honored precincts a persistent misconduct had so justly forfeited."

Instead of making any direct reply, the old gentleman stared at me with goggling eyes. He smote the table a blow with his fist so that the plates jumped and clattered.

"Jeremiah and the prophets!" he cried. "It was *born* in him!"

I hope this tribute may have been not altogether undeserved (a real talent for the proper spoken or written rendition of thought being always to some degree native)—at all events, I did not stop to acknowledge it at the time. Instead, I again levelled my finger at the completely confounded Fentriss. "Do you know what this arch-villain, this arch-hypocrite, perpetrated upon you during the watches of the night?"

"Know what he did for us!" exclaimed the old gentleman, warmly; "I do know — for God's sake take off your nightcap! — I do know what this gallant, this heroic youth has done for us!"

"Nay," quoth I.

"He saved my life and Sylvia's, too, and our purses, besides, at the risk of his skin!"

"Nay," quoth I.

"He rescued us from the largest and bloodiest band of brigands that ever took the road. Know what he did for us!"

"Nay," quoth I.

"*Nay!*" echoed Miss Sylvia, her eyes sparkling exceedingly. "Do you mean to deny his heroism? He scorns a reply and has little need to make one, seeing that my father and I were witnesses to what he did! So, 'Nay' to your heart's content, Mr. Sudgeberry!" Here she laughed, then went on, somewhat breathlessly: "But there *was* a question he might have answered long ago; yet would not, until this very morning. Can you believe the wretch would be so proud? He was determined not to satisfy me upon it till I put the question to him myself! And that was because — so he swears — because, when he came to tell me without questioning, I refused him the chance and ran off to ride with you, instead. Now, see if you can help me to discover whether or no I believe this answer of his, Mr. Sudgeberry"—she laughed again—"though, of course, 'twas a very minor point, and I never cared about it or gave the affair any consideration. The impertinent declares that when they shouted for his toast, at that wicked supper in town, he would not pronounce a lady's name where some were in wine, yet would not, so he farther swears" —still laughing, she blushed the deepest I ever saw—"would not drain his glass to any but one, and so took for his toast the name of that one's favorite color. Mr. Sudgeberry," she asked, her eyes sparkling even more than before, "would you believe his explanation if you were—that one?"

"Nay," quoth I.

"Mayhap not," she laughed, "yet I vow she finds it harder to forgive his pride, which was so hateful a thing that he waited to save her life before he *would* explain it!"

"Nay," quoth I.

"What! What!" rejoined Mr. Gray. "Why, sir, there were squadrons of 'em, and single-handed he engaged them in the noblest battle ever fought, and, what is more, he beat 'em off, like the lion that he is!"

"Nay!" I cried. "Aged man, this only shows how completely you are his dupe and how dangerously you are deceived in him. Look at him! Behold the shame and terror marked upon him!"

I pointed to Fentriss, who now turned helplessly away from every glance, his face struck white with pallor.

"Thou hypocrite!" I exclaimed, addressing myself to him. "Thou hypocrite! Tremble, for thy baseness is discovered and thy folly proven. Know, to thy discomfiture, that the landlord hath confessed his own villany, to which thy wickedness persuaded him, and stands here ready to tell the tale to this trusting old man and his daughter. Tremble before their righteous wrath, and prostrate thyself before mine. Scorn is all we have for thee; contempt is all thy portion!" I concluded, with force and majesty, despite being forced to sneeze almost continuously.

"Heaven save us!" said old Mr. Gray, impatiently. "What is all this folderol?"

Miss Sylvia's laughter had ceased abruptly: she turned to William, fixing her eyes upon him with a startled look, yet one which remained steadfastly upon him; nor did she take more than a sidelong cognizance of me, but from this moment forth remained unwaveringly observant of William, while her blushes faded and gave way to a pallor which increased till it matched his own. He was fully conscious of that earnest regard of hers, though he dared not meet it, but stood almost with his back to her, his head sinking lower and lower, and his fingers wandering aimlessly among his ruffles.

There was a long silence; then she asked, in a low voice, tremulous but clear:

"What is your accusation, Mr. Sudgeberry, if you please?"

"For Heaven's sake, what would you be

at, man?" echoed her senile parent. "Out with it!"

I began with a few brief remarks on the nature of deception, its growth and fruits in the human soul, offering some general allusions to the devastating effects of the art when employed upon and practised against innocent maidens and, especially, aged men, whereat old Mr. Gray, not having recovered from the shaking-up of his nerves, waxed very impolite, and William Fentriss, with a stifled groan, cried out, "For God's sake, man, say it and have done!" Forthwith, I proceeded to go over the events of the night, exposing in its entirety the diabolical plot by which we had suffered so much, and I forced a corroboration of each detail from the landlord, who squeezed out his testimony with extreme reluctance, groaning and apologizing to Fentriss with every word.

At last Mr. Gray broke out almost in a scream. "Not a real attack!" he vociferated. "No genuine battle! You are mad, Sudgeberry—mad as the worst in Bedlam! Why, sir, the sword-play was magnificent, and it sounded like a dozen blacksmiths hammering upon four anvils apiece; while as for the howling and firing—"

"Tell him," I bade the landlord, sternly, "tell him whether it was or was not a feigned attack, all planned to harry, and perhaps injure, himself and his daughter, in order that your accomplice yonder might gain their favor by the postures of a hero."

"No, no," protested Hoag. "There was no chance any one should be injured or hurt; and as for Mr. Fentriss, why, it was a wild thing to do, I admit, but every one who is acquainted with him or his reputation knows very well that where the danger is real, he is there to confront it twice as soon as—"

"Answer the question and no more. Was the attack feigned, and was it planned by yon crestfallen youth?"

"No more by him than by Mr. O'Donnell, now. Nay, I think Mr. O'Donnell did more—"

"Was it a feigned attack?" I interrupted,

wrathfully. "If it was real and genuine, then you were taken red-handed, and it is a case for the law — and you may know the end of that for you. Answer the question!"

"But the sword-play—" Mr. Gray began.

"Undeceive this trusting man!" I commanded.

"Well, then," said Hoag, with a piteous glance at William, "I—I—it was only a jest —we no more than made a noise, once we had the chaise stopped, and—and—"

"Go on, sir!"

"As for the sword-play, it was just two up and two down, and the shooting was only powder and no ball, up in the air, too, and—"

"Enough!" I exclaimed. "And now, thou discovered reprobate"—I addressed myself in conclusion to Fentriss — "thy perfidy is known to all. Go! Hide thy head in some obscure place where repentance may avail thee. Go in shame and discomfiture, and presume not to return where the eyes of this old man, his daughter, or myself shall again behold thy deceptions, or our ears be assailed with thy lies. Go!"

There was silence. Mr. Gray, dazed, with purple face, sank into a chair, breathing hard. The landlord was staring at the floor with an uneasy, hang-dog look. I stood with folded arms. Miss Gray, still looking steadily at my defeated rival, spoke again in the same low, clear, tremulous voice.

"Is it true, Will?" she said.

For once the fellow's impudence had utterly deserted him. His chin was sunk in the lace at his throat; his pallor had given way to the fiery blush of shame; his hand trembled at his side. A discovered trickster has ten times the anguish of a detected criminal, and the hopelessness of this one's attitude bespoke a pain which was the fit punishment for all he had done.

After a long pause, he said, brokenly,

"Yes."

"Why have you done it?" she asked.

He turned toward her, and, without speaking or even raising his eyes, lifted his hand toward her in a slight, uncertain gesture, and then let it fall.

"Oh!" she exclaimed, as sure of his meaning as if he had spoken. "You dare to tell me you did this for me! You chanced killing the horse-boys; you ruined my father's chaise and his hope of salvation—according to Mr. Sudgeberry. You risked frightening me to death—and nearly did it! Behold the condition to which you have brought your confederate, the landlord—and look at what is left of Mr. Sudgeberry! As for yourself, you took the chances of what has happened to you—detection and disgrace. Mr. Fentriss, do you dare to ask me," she cried, raising her voice—"do you dare beg me to believe that you have committed these atrocities for me?"

He tried to speak but could not; he only lifted his hand again, despairingly, and dropped it to his side.

"You must tell me better than that," said she, going very close to him.

He raised his head and met her eyes humbly, wretchedly. For once not an ounce of jauntiness was left in him; every vestige of his gay bearing was gone; even desperation had vanished; and only despair remained. My vigilance had brought him, at last, to the utter humiliation he deserved, and he afforded a spectacle wherein I read some pleasurable things for myself, as well as a warning example to the frivolous.

"Yes," he answered, finally, his voice shaking, "I did. I would have done more than that—and shall, if I get the chance!"

At this point, precisely, occurred the most astonishing event of my whole life. It happened with a necromantic suddenness that caused me at first to think my eyes gone wrong, reproducing a distorted and unreal vision, for, all at once, the cherry ribbons seemed to lie on William's shoulder. But mine orbs of vision were not distraught.

The lady had flung herself into William's arms.

"What!" cries she. "Then you must just have me! A man who would do all that for a kind word from me deserves ten thousand of them from ten thousand times a finer creature than ever I shall be! But, since you want *me*—"

With that the landlord gives a whoop and bolts from the room. I sat me down in a chair beside Mr. Gray. He seemed quite helpless, though he was able to waggle his head and make some weakish whisperings, symbolic of his darkened mind, with his lips, which I heard as one hears a sound in a dream. Miss Gray and William paid us no attention whatever.

"Nay," she said to him, with a tone of raillery so tender I could only conclude that she had been bewitched, "I was harsh to both of us, mayhap—a little; but you must never dream it was because I cared about your toasting 'Cherry.' Tell me where she lives, Will."

"Wherever Sylvia Gray abides," he answered, "that's where 'Cherry' dwells, my dear! And you know it very well."

"Do I? In truth, it did come over me, in a way, one day in the autumn after you had gone, Will, that perhaps you had meant me and the ribbons—but I don't believe it. I'll *never* believe it, *nev*—"

Here William interrupted her.

"Dearest Cherry!" he said; and may I be relegated, upon my decease, to the unquenchable conflagration, if he did not kiss her with me looking on! Her father was there, too.

I pondered upon her words. She said he must have her because he had done so much to get her. Now, I had lost my sleep; I had spent half the night crawling on hands and knees through the cold snow, falling into ditches and nigh drowning; devastating my every garment on a prickly hedge; I had been shot at once as a hippopotamus, and later fired into at close range, my nightcap burned full of holes, and my face blackened as a negro's by the discharge of a bell-mouthed blunderbuss; I had been choked, gagged, and buried in snow; the heaviest innkeeper in the colonies had leaped hither and thither upon me and had sat for a long time on my head. Heaven knows what I had *not* borne for her that night — and yet she said that William Fentriss had done so much to get her!

As I have said, there are some questions upon which the final dictum can only be, "I do not understand." Thus it was in the present instance. The whole affair was so incomprehensible as to bring about a sort of dizziness in me.

The inexplicable pair turned to us at last.

"Merry Christmas, gentlemen!" cried Fentriss, while Miss Gray greeted both her father and me with a smile of incomparable sauciness.

"We forgot you were there!" said she.

I rose.

"William," said I, "I have one favor to ask you. It is that you will tell me why you desired my society on this journey."

"I thought we might fall in with them," he replied, waving his hand toward the others, "and I thought, if we did, that you and Mr. Gray would enjoy each other's comp—"

It happened that at this moment Mr. Gray recovered his voice.

"William," he exclaimed, between his daughter's kisses, for she had sidled over to him and seated herself upon his knee, "I'll never forgive you as long as I live! Never!"

At this opposition to their marriage I looked to see the couple betray signs of distress. On the contrary, they both laughed merrily. Next, the old gentleman reached out, as well as he could for his daughter's clinging to him, and laid both hands on William's shoulders.

"William," he said, "you're a wild, rantankerous lad, but I like you, and I am glad!"

These words, directly contradicting what he had just said, and all expressions of his sentiments aforetime, were so extraordinary that, what with them and Miss Sylvia's marvellous behavior, and the cold I had caught, my head spun till I scarce knew if I stood on my feet or, inverted, upon it. The mysteries of the morning were complete.

For the first time (and the only time, I think I may claim) in my life, I was nonplussed beyond the power of expression; I was incapable of speech; what is more, I had nothing whatever to say. Without a word I walked toward the door. As I did so, old Mr. Gray's jaw fell, and he broke off in the middle of a hearty laugh over the attack on the chaise (which he now appeared to regard in a humorous light!) and began to look at me in a strange, fascinated way, while I, still uttering not one syllable, bowed silently to each of the three and, sneezing slightly, left the room.

After I had shut the door, I heard him drop into a chair and gasp.

I was so bewildered as to care little for one more mystery, and I ordered Hoag to prepare a bed for me in another part of the house, for I had made up my mind to complete my disturbed slumbers by sleeping until noon, when I should once more proceed homeward, upon the back of my misused Jeremiah.

Half an hour later I found myself dropping off to sleep between the warm, dry sheets, when I heard the chaise galloping out of the inn yard, and William and Sylvia and the old gentleman sending back a chorus of Merry Christmases to the people of the inn. Their voices rang out cheerily, particularly Sylvia's—sounding as merry as the silver chatter of the sleigh-bells that now began to jingle by.

One of my last drowsy thoughts, before slumber overcame me, was that I had been fortunate, indeed, not to have carried farther with so fickle a creature, a maiden who was overheard confessing her affection for one man in August, yet threw herself (without any expressions of regret) into the arms of another on Christmas morning! I remembered with symptoms of pleasurable anticipation the intelligent and appreciative Miss Amelia Robbins. If she was to win what Miss Sylvia's eccentricity had lost, that could be esteemed no fault of mine.

I omitted to repeat my customary oration from the classics, and, as I drifted comfortably into a sound slumber to the jingle of the Christmas sleigh-bells, I determined (in spite of the seeming light-mindedness of such a request) that, when I called at the Robbinses', next day, I would ask Miss Amelia to wear, now and again, a bunch of cherry ribbons, that being a color becoming to women.

THE END

Tarkington, Booth, 1869-
1946.
Cherry

DATE DUE

A8113	12 JA '73		
PZ 7/52			
FEB 13 1987			
JUN 28 2001			
GAYLORD			PRINTED IN U.S.A.